PRAISE FOR REBEKAH'

FIT

"I felt satisfied by a complete story at the end, and would highly recommend this to anyone looking for a fun, relatable contemporary romance." - Elisa Verna, *Romantic Times Book Reviews (TOP PICK REVIEW)*

SATED

"…I LOVED IT. The book was respectful of geeks, people with disabilities, people of color, and the BDSM community, and it was informative and entertaining, and it was funny." - Carrie S, *Smart Bitches Trashy Books*

TREASURE

"This story is rich yet beguiling, magnificent yet down to earth, and intriguing yet heartwarmingly human." – J.J., *Rainbow Book Reviews*

SO SWEET

"Reading this novella made me happy. I'm definitely looking forward to more." - LimeCello, *Heroes & Heartbreakers*

AT HER FEET

"Indeed, the more I read *At Her Feet* I came to realize that it is the best and most original book that I have read in any genre for a very long time." – Jim Lyon, *The Seattle PI*

HAVEN

REBEKAH
WEATHERSPOON

BOOKS BY REBEKAH

BEARDS & BONDAGE
Haven

THE FIT TRILOGY
Fit
Tamed
Sated

SUGAR BABY NOVELLAS
So Sweet
So Right
So For Real

VAMPIRE SORORITY SISTERS
Better Off Red
Blacker Than Blue
Soul To Keep

STAND ALONE TITLES
The Fling
At Her Feet
Treasure

For my family and friends,
who helped me find my way out of the woods.

CHAPTER ONE

SHEP

I can barely sleep. The feel of her, her scent. The sounds she makes. They still linger all around me. Even after two showers and five hours of travel. I'm never disappointed with my annual trips to Mistress Evelyn's. She and her husband are selling the place soon, but thank fuck they are selling to one of their dedicated switches and his new wife. The doors to The Club will remain open and my membership intact. And she'll still be unattached. My pet. My Meegan. I roll over and reach over Titus for my phone. Just one text and our session will be over until we meet up again next year.

My screen lights up my darkened bedroom. Titus whines, sick of my shit, and moves to the foot of my bed. He's been with the neighbors, two miles down the wooded trail for the last few days. Jad and May-Bell are saints. They know a man like me living alone in the mountains has needs. Even if they only make themselves painfully apparent once a year.

My eyes instinctively go to the various unread alerts dotting my screen. My work emails can wait for the morning. My thumb skips right over the seven and zero back lit on the red dot. I open my text messages. Mistress Evelyn received my proper and humble thanks before I caught my flight back to Sacramento. The rest of the gang wished me safe travels and sincere hopes that I won't stay away for so long. But they know the deal. I'll be back in another three hundred some odd days. I click on my messages and hit Meegan's name.

Are you in bed, pet?

Her response is immediate.

I am. I miss you, though.
Come back.

Soon, sweetheart. Soon.
Now give me a proper goodnight.

Goodnight my delicious,
delightfully rugged mountain king.

I smile, my cock throbbing in my thermals. I have to give it a rest. For a few hours. Meegan rode me raw. There's no need for me to jack off for at least a week. Another text bubble pops up.

It's Marcos.

I chuckle at the smiling emoji he sends along. Titus huffs and shifts again. "Sorry, boy." I reach for his thick fur and give him a comforting pat.

It's time for me to tuck her in.

A picture pops up, Meegan spread out on top of pink satin sheets, her inner thighs bruised up with marks from my hands and my flogger. Her pussy lips still bright red and tender. I won't make it until the morning. I grab my cock and start stroking as I type.

> *Goodnight to you both.*
> *Take care of my girl.*

Done and done.

Another picture. Marcos's stubbled cheeks and his tongue just about to drag over her clit. Good thing I am not the jealous type. I drop my phone on my bed. I'll plug it in when I'm finished.

That's when I hear the screams.

Later, when I wash her blood off in the shower I suddenly remember the day we learned about adrenaline in my AP chemistry class. How it makes you sharp, quick, super human.

I am out of my bed and in my boots before I hear the second shriek. Titus is already off the bed and bounding out the bedroom door. Isn't even a full five seconds. My steps are thundering across my hardwood floors. The pounding comes, her shrieks louder and louder as I retrieve my shotgun. Still loaded. May-Bell has always said, when you're home, boy, keep that porch light on. You never know when a stranger will come calling in the night.

"HELP!" The single word comes clearly through the thick wood I sanded and stained with my own hands.

I nudge Titus out of the way, his panicked barks mixing with her cries, then yank the door open. A Black woman is on the other side. She tumbles into my arms, a blast of cool air surrounding her unusual warmth. Later,

I'll get a good look at her. Catalog her clean dark hair and her wide hazel eyes staring at the ceiling, the fear burned into her gaze forever. But in this moment there is only blood.

I catch her with my free hand, sure to keep a grip on my firearm.

"He's coming—he's trying—he—they killed—kill—" she gasps, tries to swallow, but chokes. No gurgling though. Just spits the blood out of her mouth and tries again. She sobs. "He was right behind—me." I look down at her hands, all cut up to shit. Down at her feet. Only one wool sock. Her other foot is dirty and bleeding. I squint out into the pitch black woods. How fast was she running? I have a motion sensor installed. Still, darkness.

A second later though, I can hear him, crunching through the underbrush. And sure enough, there he is bounding through the trees. I don't think. I shove her behind me. I feel her as she trips over Titus's hulking frame. Feel the thud as she sprawls out on the floor. I step out on the porch and swing my shotgun up to my shoulder.

"Don't fucking move!" I call out just as he breaks through the trees. The lights come on. I don't hesitate. I fire. Of course, momentarily blinded, I fucking miss. But the warning shot was enough to get his attention. More blood and dirt cover him from eyebrows to the toes of his boots. Blood covers the small knife in his hand.

"Well, well. She made it to civilization. Guess our little game is coming to an end." He eases closer.

"Please." A delicate voice whimpers behind me. "Shoot him."

"You stop and I bring you in alive," I yell. "You take another fucking step and I'll blow your fucking head off."

He raises his hands in surrender and a sick smile spreads across his face. "We could share her, man."

I'm done trying to bargain with the psycho. I mutter a prayer to myself and pull the trigger.

The adrenaline is still pumping. My priorities slide into clear focus. I keep Titus from making the situation worse by either licking this injured woman sitting on my floor (more than he already has) or by making a chew toy out of what is left of her attacker. It takes some work, but I corral him into my bedroom and lock the door.

When I come back into the great room, the woman is passed out in the threshold of my cabin. Still bleeding from a gash on her forehead, but still breathing. I grab a dish towel and my first aid kit from under the sink and do the best triage I can manage on her head and right hand, but it's clear these wounds are just a couple of many. I have to get her to the hospital.

Jad Tierney calls my house phone as I search for my keys. I tear the cordless phone off its base when I see his name flash across the caller ID.

"Were those shots I just heard?"

"Yeah. Fuck. Shit. Sorry, yes."

"You okay?"

"Yes, no. Yes. *I'm* fine. I don't know what happened. I have this woman here. She's pretty beat up. I shot the guy who was chasing her."

"Is he dead?"

I swallow, a sick sense of pride clouding my thoughts. "Yeah, he's dead. I didn't miss the second time." I find my keys on my kitchen table. "I can't wait for Reva or Kevin to get up here. I'm taking her down to QER myself. You gotta call Jerry." There was no time to wait for an ambulance crew to make it up to my place.

"Should we come over?" I hear May-Bell in the background.

"No! Absolutely not."

"Okay," Jad says, trying to call me down.

"Just stay at your place and call Jerry. And—fuck, tell him to bring backup. He shouldn't handle this by himself."

"Okay, son. Okay."

"I'll call you as soon as I can." I hang up and rush back over to the woman again. Still knocked out, but a quick check of her pulse tells me she's still kicking. I throw on my jacket—it's balls freezing outside—and then carefully pick her up and walk her out to the passenger side of my truck, doing my best to shield her view from the body sprawled out lifeless in my yard, even though her eyes are closed.

I don't drive carefully. The adrenaline is still flowing. I reverse out of my driveway, stopping only to throw open the fence at the end of my property, then I gun it down the dirt road until I reach the paved rural route. I know these mountain roads of the Paluma National Forest like the back of my hand and I know as we pass the two county cruisers, blue and whites blazing halfway down the narrow mountain road, we are still twenty minutes away from the ER in Quinten.

She moans beside me, then groans even louder when her head lolls to the side and smacks the passenger window.

"Shit."

"I… what… my head?" She reaches up and touches the makeshift bandage.

"Stay with me, okay?" I glance over at my passenger then back at the road. "We're gonna be there soon."

That doesn't seem to help. She starts shaking. Blood loss or shock or just straight-up fear, I have no clue, but I'm going to get her help. She says something. It sounds more like a squeak than actual words.

"What was that?"

"My brother," she whispers, then lets out a guttural sob. "They killed my brother."

Fucking shit. "Are you sure?"

She nods, though it looks more like a shiver. "I'm pretty sure. I just—I just ran. He told me to run."

"No, you did the right thing. You should have run. You made it. You're gonna be okay." I grope for the CB radio and switch over to the emergency channel, ignoring the blood that's already dried on my hand. This is all information that Sheriff Bingham needs to know.

I take a deep breath. "It's Shep. There might be another victim near the pass trail. Over."

"10-4, Shep," The voice of my childhood friend Abigail comes cracking back through the speaker. "Jerr and Will are on their way. Over."

I glance back at the woman, a second too long. I almost overcorrect and drive us off the road. "Shit! Sorry. I'm sorry. You said they. There was more than one of them? More than one of them attacked you?" I ask her. Nothing. "Come on, darling. Stay with me."

She doesn't respond, but her shoulders shake. Another strange noise bubbles up. At least she's still conscious.

I hit the button on the radio again. "Shep again. Tell the boys to be on the lookout. There might be another perp. He might be armed. Over."

More crackling. "Copy that. Over."

"Can you tell me your name?" I ask.

She answers me, but I can't hear her weakened voice over the sound of my engine.

"I'm sorry, darling. Can you speak up a little?"

"Claudia. My name is Claudia." Definitely crying.

"I'm Shep, Claudia. Sorry we couldn't have met under better circumstances. Normally, I'd hug you. But I don't want to jostle you any more than I already have. Can you hang in there with me a little longer?"

No response.

"Can you tell me what hurts?"

"My head," she mutters.

"Okay, good, good. What else?"

"My feet hurt. My foot. I don't have any shoes on."

"Yeah, you showed up with no shoes. We'll get you shoes. Don't worry. Tell me what else hurts."

"My side. He kicked me—a couple times. And I—I can't see very well." I glanced over again. I didn't have time to wipe all the blood away. It was definitely in her eyes.

"They'll get you cleaned up. I promise. Do you want to hold my hand?" I offer, dropping my radio mic on my center console.

She doesn't answer, she just reaches for me. Her fingertips are freezing, but she holds on.

"Just stay with me," I say more to myself. Still, Claudia squeezes my fingers.

Reva and Eartha are waiting with Dr. Spring and a stretcher as soon as I pull into the ambulance bay. I hop out and run around to help them open the door.

"Jesus, Shep!" Eartha gasps as she looks me up and down. I realize I'm still not wearing a shirt. My chest and my pants are covered in Claudia's blood.

"I'm fine. I'm fine. I'm not bleeding. Help her." I rip open the passenger door and ease her into my arms and onto the stretcher.

"What happened?" Dr. Spring asks as we race inside the ER's double doors.

"Someone attacked her in the woods and I think her brother. I passed Will and Jer, but you gotta send an ambulance up for the brother. I think they were off Grafton's Pass. I didn't see him."

"Thank you, Shep. You did good. We got it from here."

I nod and drop back, but Claudia reaches for me. "Shep," she says weakly.

"Don't worry, hun," Dr. Springs says in her soothing voice. "He'll be right here. Don't worry."

I wait in the hallway until they disappear with Claudia through another set of doors. I shove my hands in my pockets and realize that I don't have my keys or my phone. They are both in my truck, which is still sitting in the ambulance bay. I jog outside and park my truck in the parking lot, ignoring the sounds of sirens in the otherwise quiet night. Back inside, the emergency waiting room is quiet.

I can't sit. I'm calm, but my heart's still pounding. There's ringing in my ears. I start pacing. I keep looking at my hands. It's definitely shock.

"Hey man." I look up at Todd Logan, QER's worst orderly. There was a time when Todd kicked my ass for fun, but my growth spurt put an end to that. "Eartha told me to give you this." He has a set of scrubs in his hand. "What the fuck happened?"

"I don't know."

"Who'd you kill?" He laughs. I don't. "Oh shit. You fucking killed someone?"

"How about we do this some other time," I say.

"You brought in the stab wounds? Did you stab her?"

"Todd!" We both look up as his grandmother comes back through the swinging doors. "Is your shift over?"

"No, ma'am." She rips the blue shirt out of his hand and nods down the other hall. "Scoot."

"I gotta hear this story, man," he says as he starts walking backwards down the hall.

"Don't pay attention to him," Miss Fern says with a smile.

"Did you see her?" I ask as I finally sit.

"They're still working on her now, but I think she'll be okay. She's fighting. You want to tell me what happened?" Fern Logan, unlike her shitty ass grandson is beloved by the whole county. She kept me in casseroles for a year after my grandfather passed. It isn't a matter of whether or not I feel like I *can* rehash the last two hours of my life. It's more like I respect Miss Fern enough to dredge it all up again. I tell her every detail.

"You saved her life."

"Maybe. She—yeah. Her brother might still be out there though. She said he told her to run. He might be dead."

"Try not to think about that, sweetheart. You did what you could and that was a whole lot."

"Yeah." I look down at my hands again.

"We haven't had one of these in a while, but just hang tight. You're gonna have to talk to Jerry. About all of this." I look up into her milky green eyes. She nods down at my hands. They are shaking. So is my leg. I've known Jerry as long as I've known anyone in Quentin County, but I should probably get my shit together before I sit down to talk to the head of the Sheriff's department.

"I know," I say.

"You want some coffee?"

"I'll grab it."

"Nonsense. You've had a hell of a night. Just hang tight. I'll check in on her and then I'll grab you something to drink."

"Thank you."

I wait. Fern comes back with coffee. They are finishing up with Claudia. They'll have more news in a few minutes, she tells me. A woman comes in with a feverish baby. I try not to let the look on her face when she does a double take in my direction bother me too much. After Fern gets the mother and her baby situated, Fern checks on Claudia again. She's out of surgery. Even though I'm not family, she sneaks me back.

Dr. Spring is waiting for us outside of her room. "We gave her something for the pain so she's a little woozy, but she's fighting sleeping. She's a tough one for sure."

"I'm seeing that," I say.

Fern winks at me, then ushers me inside of the room. I hesitate until she and Dr. Spring are out of sight before I enter all the way. Then I zip up my jacket and shove my hands in my pockets. I sit in the shitty plastic chair beside her bed.

Fuck, she's banged up. Even with the blood and dirt finally washed away from her golden brown skin, it is clear as day that piece of shit had definitely tried to kill Claudia. Her head and her right hand are bandaged, and her left foot all the way up to her calf. There are scrapes and scratches all over her and her left eye is already starting to swell up.

"Hey."

"Hey." A fat tear runs down her cheek. I want to wipe it away, but my hands. "My brother. Miles. Did they find him?" Her words are a little slurred, but loud enough for me to make them out.

"Haven't heard anything yet, but as soon as I see the sheriff I'll find out for you."

"They killed him." More fat tears.

"Shhh." I slide closer, pissed for some reason that I can't touch her. I barely know her. I don't *know* her at all. "It's gonna be okay. You're safe now."

"I ran. I just left him."

"Claudia. Look at me." She listens, turning her head the little bit that she can. Her hazel eye, the one that isn't swelling shut, is big and bloodshot, but is the most beautiful eye I am pretty sure I've ever seen. "I'm gonna stay here with you until we find out where your brother is. Okay? I'm not going anywhere."

She glares at me and then squints a little. "What's your name again?"

"Shep. Shep Olsen."

Her eyes close. "Thank you, Shep. For shooting that guy. I—I can't repeat what he said to me."

"You don't have to. Not to me. Save it for the cops when you're ready. Okay?"

"Okay."

"Just try and sleep," I say.

"I don't think I can."

"Well I'm gonna sit here with you anyway."

"'Kay."

I think she might be able to hold out, but either the drugs or the exhaustion take over. I watch her sleep for over two hours. Miss Fern comes back with more coffee and Eartha comes to check on Claudia's vitals and mine. I can't stop shaking. Caffeine and shock don't mix. She says I'll be fine, but I should probably switch to water. I just want Claudia to be okay. I want them to find her fucking brother. Alive and well.

A while later, I hear my name.

"Shep." I look up and see Jerry standing in the hallway with Dr. Spring. He nods toward me and then toward the exit. "Let's go for a walk."

I stand, look at Claudia one more time, then follow Jerry out and down the hall. Across town to the sheriff's station.

CHAPTER TWO

"I can't say we're gonna make this quick," Jerry says as he holds the station door open for me.

"I'm not in a hurry."

"Come on this way." I follow Jerry through two sets of heavy steel doors with mesh enforced pocket windows, down a short hallway past two more doors into what looks like the interrogation room. The last time I'd set foot in the sheriff's station, I'd been there to tell Will that his wife had lost her phone and she'd call him as soon as she got home. The last time, I wasn't covered in someone else's blood.

"Do I need a lawyer?" I ask when he closes the door behind me.

"Do you want one?"

"No. I didn't do anything wrong."

"You let me know if you change your mind."

In walks one of the sheriff's deputies with a small digital camera. A young guy with white blond hair and huge eyes. I'd never seen him before.

"We're just gonna take a few pictures," Jerry says. "Just stand against the wall right there."

I hold still, moving when they say, letting them photograph every inch of me.

"We're gonna have to take your clothes and your boots," Jerry says when they finish. "Taylor will get you something to wear." The deputy flashes me a half smile, almost an apology, then walks out of the room. Jerry takes off his jacket and hangs it on the back of the metal chair across from me and then hits record on the little device that is already sitting on the table. I listen as he rattles off our names, the date, the time, and that he is questioning me about the double homicide near Grafton's Pass.

"Did you find the brother?"

"Uh… I can't comment on that at the moment. Let's you start at the beginning. You just got back in town today? Yesterday." The sun is still down, but it is definitely morning.

"Yeah, I was visiting some friends down in Los Angeles."

"And we can contact them if we need to?"

I think for a moment, then answer truthfully. I am pretty sure the whole county knows about my annual pilgrimage, they just don't know the particulars. "I was with an Evelyn Baker and some of our mutual friends. I'll leave her contact information."

"Good. So I've got one dead up at GPSite Five and one dead at your property and one in recovery. Tell me what happened."

I tell Jerry everything from the moment I heard Claudia's first scream, trying not to focus on the fact that Site Five is two miles from my house. Downhill.

"And how do you know the young lady's name?"

"I was trying to keep her talking in the truck. She told me. Your guy at the campsite should be her brother. At least that's what she said."

We stop for a few moments when Taylor comes back with a pair sheriff's department sweats, a t-shirt and a pair of fishing boots.

"The pants are probably a little short."

"It's fine. And don't worry about the boots. I have sneakers in my truck." I change and let him throw my thermals, my boots and my jacket into some evidence bags. "My phone might have some blood on it. It's out in the truck."

"Her blood?" Jerry asks.

"Yeah."

"You hold on to it for now." Jerry excuses Taylor with a nod and we continue.

"She said there are two of them."

"Yeah she told them that at the hospital. One attacked her and one attacked her brother. We're out looking for him now. We checked on Titus too. He wasn't amused but he's fine. We'll let you back up there so you can get him soon."

"But I can't stay there? At my house."

Jerry shakes his head. "Jad and May-Bell are waiting for you. You can stay there until we clear the scene. What else can you tell me?"

Just then we hear a commotion outside of the room. Taylor throws open the door.

"Jer—they got him! He's over at QER."

"They shoot him?" Jerry grunts then stands and grabs his jacket.

"No. He was running across 70 and Will clipped him with the cruiser, but he's alive."

"Good. Don't leave town, Shep."

"I won't." I watch Jerry as he stops the recording, then follow him back to the front of the station. The radio and the phone are going crazy. Outside I dig my beat-up running shoes out of the backseat and watch Jerry as he throws on his lights and bolts toward the hospital. I sit in my truck for a while, waiting for the sun to come up. Jerry still hasn't come back by the time I figure I should move.

I take my time driving back up to my house, making a mental list of everything I need to take for at least the next few days. And I know even though I can't stay at my place, I have to get Titus. Crime scene be damned. I'm stopped at the open gate to my property and a Sheriff's deputy escorts me up the rest of the way on foot and follows me in my back door.

The whole front is taped off. There's still a body in my yard. Titus is spooked, but happy to see me. I grab some clothes and some other shit like my toothbrush. My laptop and my camera are still packed. I grab both bags and my drives. Then I grab my dog.

The drive over to the Tierneys' takes its usual ten minutes. I could have walked it if I'd cut through the woods. Doesn't seem like the best idea at the moment. Like Jerry said, May-Bell is waiting up for me. Light pours out the front door, illuminating her round frame before I can cut off my engine.

"Shep." May-Bell's face tells me everything about the way I look as I walk up the front steps.

"I'm okay."

"Come in. Come in." I don't realize how cold I am until I set foot inside their house. The heat from the roaring fire warms my whole right side.

"You want something to eat? We have some scraps for this one too." She reaches down and scratches Titus's chin.

"No thank you, but a shower would be great."

"Sure. Come on, honey. Let's distract you while your dad gets cleaned up." She ushers Titus into the kitchen and gives him a full bowl of shit that would probably stop his heart if I fed him that way regularly. Their own ancient, extremely deaf bloodhound is passed out near the fireplace.

"Where's Jad?" I ask.

"He went out to help. You know retirement doesn't mean a thing to him. He has his gun though."

"Good. I think they caught the other guy."

"There were two?! You know what? Let me stop rattling on. You look worse than all hell. Come on."

I follow May-Bell into the bathroom. She grabs me a towel from the linen shelves I'd helped Jad install when he redid their place.

"You get clean and I'll make you something to calm your nerves." I didn't realize, but my hands are still shaking.

"Thanks."

When she's gone, I strip out of my borrowed clothes that I'll probably ask her to burn, and step in the shower. The hot spray hits me center chest. I grab the Irish Spring and scrub until my hands are almost raw.

May-Bell doesn't hassle me for the details when I get out. Just hands me her version of a hot toddy and points me toward the couch.

"Didn't think you two would get that beast up the mountain or in the front door," she says, smiling at the massive sectional I'm sitting on. "Plenty of room for you to put your feet up." She hands me a quilt, then settles on the far end of the chaise with her own blanket. Neither of us are going to get much sleep.

*

Going to The Corner Diner in the morning is a mistake, but after the shitty night we'd all had, I want to give Jad some time to regroup with May-Bell alone. Plus the diner has the strongest coffee in town. I want to be awake. After May-Bell helps me scrub most of the blood off my front seat, I head down the mountain and go right to the diner.

I'm too out of it from two hours of sleep and what May-Bell pretends wasn't a half fifth of whiskey to expect *anything*, but everyone stops talking and eating the second I walk in the door. I take off my skull cap, and scratch my beard as I approach the counter.

"Don't mind them all staring at you. We haven't had a hero in here since Eartha came back from Iraq," Connie says as she places a fresh cup in front of me. "Your usual?" she asks.

"Yeah. Please. Tell Paul double the eggs and the bacon if he's got them."

"We're never short on eggs or bacon." She winks at me, then pats my hand before she moves on. The regular commotion of the diner resumes and I soak in the white noise as I work on my first cup of coffee and then another. I'm almost finished with my Woodsman's Special when Will comes in and sits down beside me.

"Connie, give me whatever you got that's hot and ready."

"Just pulled the first pies out. Is peach okay?"

"Throw in some hot chocolate and that's the breakfast of champions."

I keep my eyes trained forward while he makes himself comfortable on the stool beside me. I know looking at Will might open a door I'm not in the right frame of mind to open, maybe not now or ever.

"I know Jer already asked, but I think you should reconsider," Will says quietly.

"Reconsider what?"

"Joining the force."

I actually laugh. That draws plenty of attention.

"After last night, you've got more on the job experience than any of us new boys," Will says.

"Not sure you want any of the experience I had last night."

"Maybe not, but clearly if it hadn't been for you—"

"Not necessary, man," I say, cutting him off with a shake of my head.

"I'm just saying. I was there when Jerry finally interviewed the girl. You were quick on your feet, quick with the trigger, and you saved her life and who knows who else's."

"Hmm?" I finally look him. "What does that mean?"

"We got a call right as I was leaving the station. These boys might have a few more bodies on them. All in the last six months. I'm just guessing, but they were probably escalating. So like I said, that was some good shit, Shep."

"I heard you brought him in, Will. That's not nothing."

"Yeah I'll take the collar, but I'd rather it hadn't been a complete accident. Clipped that asshole too, though. Kurt Milligan. Confessed to everything. Douglas Smith is the guy you dropped."

"Milligan still up in the hospital?" I ask.

"Nah. He was fine. I bruised him up, but that was it. They cleaned him up and—"

"Most of the blood wasn't his?"

"Bingo."

"God, this is a fucking mess." I push my plate away and pull on my hat.

"You heading back to Jad's?"

"I have to pick up a few things from the market, but I was thinking about it."

"Well, she's up. And she asked about you. I'm sure Fern told her day crew that you get visiting privileges."

The sudden ache in my chest make no sense. I don't know Claudia, but I do want to check in on her. I have to make sure she's okay. I feel responsible for her.

I throw down a twenty, then clap a hand on Will's shoulder. "Later."

He nods, shoving a big chunk of pie in his mouth.

I fucking hate hospitals. The smells, the sounds, the bright lights, and the washed out walls. To me they all signify the reality of death. And it doesn't mean shit to me that babies are born there. I was born on a boat. Babies are fucking resilient.

The night before I'd been reasonably distracted. I hadn't paid attention to any of these things, the sounds, the smells, but they are harder to ignore when I'm being shuffled between the emergency room and where they've moved Claudia in a different part of the hospital.

When I'm finally directed to the correct wing and room number, I run into Sarah. Sarah Maxwell. It's been a while. I've prayed several times that'll I'll never see her again, but a man can only be so lucky.

"Hey Shep," she says. Her voice has that tone, like a sad warning. She feels bad for me.

"You're back. When did that happen?" Sarah and I dated for a long time, but she didn't think life on the mountain suited her. More like, *my* life on the mountain didn't suit her. Last I knew she was engaged to some guy up in Portland.

Her eyebrows pull together in annoyed confusion. "A few months ago."

"You staying?"

"Looks like it." She moves her hands in a sweeping motion, indicating the fresh pair of nursing scrubs she is wearing.

"It's nice to see you," I lie. Looking at her still fucks with my chest.

"You too. And I mean that. I heard last night was pretty crazy." Without warning she steps forward and wraps her arms around my torso. She smells the same, but her flowery shampoo doesn't have the same effect on me anymore. I wrap an arm around her shoulders and pull her closer. "I'm glad you're okay," she whispers.

"Thank you."

She steps away and straightens her shirt. Then wipes her eyes. "So you're here to see our special patient."

"Yeah. I wanted to check in on her. Like you said, kind of a crazy night."

"She's been asking about you. Cliff Watson's manning the door." Of course. Ongoing murder investigation. Couldn't leave the surviving witness unattended.

"Thanks."

"But take it easy. She's really shaken up."

"Understandable." I gave her shoulder a squeeze. "I guess I'll see you around then."

"I guess you will." She holds up her now bare ring finger. I flash her a tight smile and continue down the hall. Sarah is a good girl. Too good. Not the woman for me.

When I turn the corner, I find Cliff Watson where she said he'd be.

"Visiting hours aren't until later," he says in his gravelly voice. The Watsons don't care for any of the Olsens. The feeling is mutual.

"I'll keep that in mind when I come back later to check on her," I say.

"Have it your way. You deal with Fern's wrath and Jerry's."

I roll my eyes and knock on the door that is part way open anyway. Claudia opens her eyes and looks at me.

"Hey. Hi. Is it okay if I come in?" I ask.

"Hi. Yeah." She lets out a weak cough as I step inside. "Shep."

"Yeah that's me. Wanted to come check on you."

"See how I was doing?"

"Yeah. Something like that. Do you mind if I sit?"

"No. Please. Can you pull the chair there though? It hurts when I move my head to the side too much."

"Of course." I pick up the blue chair and move it further down the length of the bed.

"It's nice to see someone who isn't in some type of uniform. One of the sheriffs told me they found my brother."

There is absolutely nothing I can say. "They didn't tell me much."

"But they talked to you?" she asks.

"Yeah."

"I owe you—"

"You don't owe me anything."

"Except my life." I look down at the pale blue hospital blanket as she opens her bandaged hand. The tips of her fingers are scratched up, but clean. And not bleeding. I gently take her hand.

"Please stay for a while," she says.

"No plans for the day." I'd already emailed my boss at the forest service and the dev guys at my other job. They know they won't be hearing much from me until I get back into my house.

"So you live on the mountain?" Claudia asks.

"I do. We don't have to talk if you don't want to. You can rest."

"You're not much of a talker?" Something in her voice makes my blood rush to all the wrong places. I shift in my seat.

"I can be."

"So you live on the mountain?" she urges again.

"Yeah, most of my life. That's my grandfather's place. But it's just me now."

"So we have something in common." I tilt my head. "It's just me too. It was just Miles and me. We lost our parents right after I graduated from college."

"Claudia—" She shakes her head a little.

"You know, I hate the woods. I hate camping. I'm a city girl. Manhattan is the place for me. But Miles just finished his residency at Stanford and he wanted to get away for a while so I flew three thousand miles to catch up with my brother, get in that sibling quality time we'd been missing so much. Some fucking getaway."

"They caught him. The guy who attacked your brother. He'll get life for this. Maybe more," I tell her.

"Good." A few tears run down the side of her face. She quickly wipes them away with a tissue she's gripping in her other hand. "Do you like it here? I didn't get to see too much of the town before we headed up the trails. It seems nice. At least the nurses are nice."

"Have the sheriff's boys been treating you alright?" I ask.

"Yeah. I got a little bit of the hysterical woman treatment, but I know they are just worried and a little out of their depth maybe. They weren't being dicks or anything though."

"I'm sure they'll let you out of here soon."

"I'm not looking forward to a six hour flight banged up like this, but it'll be nice to sleep in my own bed."

"Is there anyone you need me to call?" I don't know what makes me offer. Fern has probably made sure it was taken care of herself.

"I wasn't due back to work until Wednesday, but I told them who to look up."

"Good."

"It hasn't even hit me yet and I just miss him. I've gone months without seeing my brother, but just the idea that I'm never gonna see him again..."

"It's a lot."

"It's a lot," she says.

"When something bad would happen, my grandfather used to tell me to imagine all the ways it could have been worse."

She lets out a harsh burst of laughter. More tears stream down her face. She doesn't bother wiping them away. "Oh please. Try me."

"They could have been clowns," I say. "I've encountered some crazy shit in these woods, but never clowns."

She laughs for real this time. "Oh my god. That would have been fucking awful." She laughs a little harder, grabbing her side. "Oh my god. I wouldn't have run. I would have sprouted wings and flown the fuck out of there."

"Yeah, if I'd seen a clown when I opened my door, you would have been on your own." I chuckle a bit myself, watching her as her laughter becomes a bit more hysterical. And then it hits that point. She finally cracks. That moment I think she's been waiting for finally hits. She loses it and starts sobbing.

I look over as Cliff throws the door open, making her jump. She starts shaking.

"Jesus, dude," I say. "Just give her a second."

"Sorry," he says, realizing his mistake. He eases back, closing the door all the way.

"I know we just met, but do you want me to hold you? I'll do it, happily. I'm only asking 'cause I want it to be your choice. I figure you might do with some comforting," I say.

"Please."

There's no room on that hospital bed for me, period, but I gently move her IV stand and lift her into my lap. She lightly rests her head on my chest and cries.

CHAPTER THREE

I let Claudia cry herself out and sometime after she's snoring softly on my chest, I pass out. I don't know what time it is when shouting in the hallway jerks us both awake. Claudia grimaces and grabs her forehead.

"Shit. You okay?"

"Yeah. Just really tender."

I ease out of the bed, giving her some space to get comfortable again without me in the way.

"They are both in there?! Together?" the voice that woke me up says.

"Yeah—it seems so." That's Jerry.

"Jesus. You guys really know how to run a tight ship."

"Listen—"

I take a deep breath and move the IV stand closer to the bed as Claudia adjusts her covers. When I look up, a White man and a White woman in dark suits are standing in the doorway. Jerry's behind them, his face all puffed up and red.

"Shepard Olsen? Claudia Cade?" the woman asks.

"Yes?" we both say.

"I'm Alice Lightfoot and this is my partner, Scott Tanner. We're with the FBI. We need to speak to you."

I glance down at Claudia.

"Okay. Speak," I say.

"Shep." I look at Jerry over their shoulders and shoot him an incredulous look.

"What?"

"We need to speak to Miss Cade as well. Without you."

I glance back down at Claudia. She looks terrified, but when her fingers brush mine I realize she's trying to comfort me.

"For fuck's sake. Fine. I'll be back," I tell her.

"Actually, I don't think that would be a good idea. Miss Cade needs some time to recover," Agent Tanner says.

"Am I under arrest?"

"We'd like to talk to you first."

"Fine." I give Claudia's damaged fingers a light squeeze. "I will be back."

"Okay," she says. Her voice is weak, but there's confidence in her unbruised eye. She knows I'll be back for her.

We walk out in the hallway. Jerry follows us to the main entrance. He cuts off and walks toward his cruiser near the curb.

"Sheriff, let's see if your men can follow orders this time. She doesn't get any visitors. Hospital personnel only," Lightfoot says.

"We'll see to it." He's still red when he jumps behind the wheel and floors it. I watch Jerry speed away and try not to consider what it means that he's left me with these assholes.

"Where are you going, Mr. Olsen?" Tanner asks.

I turn around. "To my truck."

They share a look.

"Why don't we come with you. And then we'll give you a ride back to the station."

I hold in an annoyed grunt. "Sure thing."

We walk out to the visitors' lot. I see right away that May-Bell and I didn't exactly aim for precision when we were scrubbing my truck down. There's still a few specks of blood on the door.

"Can you unlock it for us?" Agent Lightfoot asks.

I unlock it remotely without taking my keys out of my pocket.

"It's a nice truck. Expected something a little more beat up for someone who lives on the mountain," Tanner says as he snaps on a pair of rubber gloves. Lightfoot is slowly walking around of the front of my Chevy.

"Yeah, rusted out classics with no heat are great when they break down in the pass," I say.

"Touché."

I watch them as they slowly inspect every inch, doing my best to keep my mouth shut. Tanner calls Lightfoot over to the passenger side. He mutters something and then she pulls out her phone.

"Yeah. We need someone down here to collect evidence from Shepard Olsen's vehicle." She pauses. "Not much. He scrubbed it pretty good, but there's still some trace evidence." She ends the call with a "Yep." Then turns to Tanner, who's taking off his gloves. "Why don't you two go have a chat?" I'll catch up with you in a bit."

Tanner nods, then turns to me with this creepy as fuck smile. "Come on. We're right over here." Right over here is back in front of the hospital's main entrance. They've left their car in a red zone. There's only a few people coming in and out of the main doors, but that's enough to get people talking. I climb into the front seat to keep the rumors that I'm the real suspect to a minimum. Tanner doesn't object.

"How do you and Miss Cade know each other?" he asks as we drive away from the hospital.

"We don't."

"No doubt you two are already bonded through this experience, but from the looks of things you seem pretty close. I saw the way she looked at you from that hospital bed. My wife isn't even that protective of me."

"That sounds like a problem between you and your wife."

"Hmm." Tanner grunts and then he laughs. He doesn't saying anything else until we're back in the Sheriff's station. We go through the whole song and dance, but this time Tanner sits me down with a video camera pointing right at me over his shoulder.

"So tell me what happened last night," he says.

"I heard screaming outside my cabin and then someone banging on my door."

"Mhmm? Go on."

"I got up, grabbed my gun and when I opened the door, Claudia—"

"Miss Cade."

"She told me her name was Claudia. You want me to be more formal?" I ask.

"I want to make sure you two aren't tangled up in this some other way."

"Tangled up how? Do you think she and I planned this? Do you think I shot the wrong guy?" I don't have time for this shit.

"I want to make sure we put the right guy away. Please continue."

"I opened the door and Claudia basically fell into my arms."

"And she was injured?"

"Yes, she was covered in blood. She said someone was chasing her—"

"Was she out of breath?"

"Yes." I sigh. I prefer Jerry's method of questioning where he barely asks any questions. "Not even thirty seconds later, the guy—the one I shot—came out of the woods."

"Did he say anything?"

"I told him not to move and he said something about how their little game had come to an end. Like he'd been hunting her." Tanner nods, then writes something down.

"Did he say anything else?"

"He said we could share her."

"And then you shot him?"

"I warned him not to come any closer and when he did, I shot him." I swallow, ignoring the fact that the kickback bruise on my shoulder is still aching.

Tanner goes on. "When was the last time you fired your weapon?"

"Maybe two months ago, down at the range."

"You ever have to use it up in the woods?"

"Just once. A bear came after my dog, but a warning shot scared it away."

"Was your dog present last night?"

"Yes."

"Did he touch either the victim or the deceased?"

"No. I shoved him into the bathroom. You can ask Jerry. He was still in the bathroom when him and the boys went up." They're not dragging Titus into this.

The door opens then and Lightfoot walks in and sits in the open chair next to Tanner. I can't wait to see who's going to be the bad cop.

"Shep," she says.

"Shepard works fine," I say.

"Shepard. What can you tell me about Miles Cade?"

"Not much. All she told me was that her brother was back at the campsite. They were both attacked and he told her to run."

"So you didn't go back down to the campsite to check on him?" Lightfoot asks, her frown adding a little extra guilt to the accusation.

"No. I had a woman who was in clear need of medical attention. She didn't mention her brother until we were halfway down the mountain."

"In your truck."

"Yes."

"From the looks of your cabin, there must have been a lot of blood in your truck. When did you clean it?" Lightfoot asks.

"This morning before I came down. I went to the diner for breakfast."

"So we have the timeline clear. You're in bed. Miss Cade shows up at your door. You fire on the deceased, then bring Miss Cade down to the emergency room in Quinten," Tanner says.

"That's it. I was at the hospital for a while and then I came here and spoke with Sheriff Bingham. I told him the same thing I'm telling you, exactly as it happened. Is there anything else? Am I under arrest?"

"No, you are not," Tanner says reluctantly, which makes no fucking sense.

"I thought they got the other guy," I reply. "I'm not sure what the problem is."

"There's no problem—" Lightfoot starts.

Tanner interrupts. "We're just in the middle of a multi-state investigation. There's evidence that Douglas Smith, the man you killed, and his accomplice are connected to a series of murders across the national parks system."

"And that's why the Feds are involved."

"That is correct."

I stand and slip my hat back on. "Well I'm not going anywhere if you have any more questions."

"Thank you. Let's see if we can get one of the deputies to give you a lift back up to the Tierneys' place. Is that where you're staying?" Tanner asks.

"Yes."

"Why don't you head back up there?"

"And what about my truck?"

"We're just giving it a good twice over," Lightfoot says. "We'll let you know when we can turn it back over to you."

"Thanks," I say, my tone dry.

Sally Morgan is on the day shift and she's waiting for me with her keys when we come out of the interrogation room. I hate seeing this look on her face. She's nervous as hell. Most action she's seen since joining the force is a hiker who broke his ankle.

"You ready, Shep?" she says, her eyes darting between me and Tanner, who thinks I can't be trusted to walk to the front of the station.

"Yeah. Thanks for the lift," I say as she leads the way outside. "You okay?" I ask when she's behind the wheel.

"Yeah. I'm fine. It's just—I wasn't expecting this when I came into work this morning. I mean, I'm in uniform, but…"

"I get it."

"I feel like—I feel like I should quit."

"Hey." I look over and see Sally is dashing tears from under her eyes. "Jer told me I would answer the phones, direct traffic, and poke Mr. Harmon to make sure he's breathing when they have to stick him in the drunk tank."

"Here, pull over." I was sure she could see, but she was starting to hyperventilate and it was starting to rain. She doesn't need to swerve into oncoming traffic. The shoulder is clear up ahead and she stops and smacks the hazard light. I reach up and turn it off.

"Someone will think your cruiser's broken down."

"Right." Sally lets out a shaky breath, then she turns to me. "They sent me up to your house this morning. The body wasn't even covered. Jerry told me there was a body, I just didn't expect it to be out in the open like that. I'm not cut out for this."

"Don't quit, Sal. Really. This will be over soon. And I promise I won't shoot anybody else as long as I live on the mountain," I say, then nudge her shoulder a little with my closed fist.

When she looks over at me her eyes are still watery. "Oh Shep. I'm sorry."

"It's okay, really."

"I should quit anyway. You're going through all this, I'm just a spectator and I'm crying all over you. Let me get you back up to Jad's."

"Actually, can you drop me back at the hospital?"

"I can't, Shep. Strict orders. I have to take you back to the Tierneys'." I can hear what she's not saying. The last thing she needs is to get chewed out by Jerry or the FBI just because I'm not good at following instructions. She'd quit for sure.

"Yeah. Okay. Let's head up before it starts coming down harder."

She checks her mirrors, then pulls back on the empty road. "Gosh, I can't believe it's raining again."

"Hope they got all the evidence they need," I say, more to myself, as I look out the window.

"I think they did and Milligan confessed."

"Why were they grilling me then?" I ask.

"The Feds don't trust us. They always expect us to foul things up, but Jerry was thorough and they took pictures of every square inch this morning. Those should hold up fine in court. If this goes to trial."

We slowly make our way up toward the Tierneys. I try to look up my road as it forks off the main, but it's tapped off and blocked by an unmarked sedan and another sheriff's cruiser.

"It shouldn't be more than a day now and you should be able to go home. This rain." It was pouring now. When we reach the house, the gravel drive is already riddled with trickling streams and forest debris.

"Things will get back to normal around here soon," I say, trying to reassure Sally.

"And if it doesn't, I heard Margee Fulton is retiring soon. I've always wanted to be a children's librarian."

"You'd be great at that," I say, mustering the bit of a smile I have in reserve. "But don't hang up your badge just yet."

She thanks me as I climb out of the car.

When I come in the door, Titus is all over me. He doesn't like change. He also loves the rain. I nudge him back to keep him inside. Their bloodhound, Fox, is awake but not so interested in me or why there's all this commotion in their home.

"There's food warming in the oven," May-Bell offers. I'm too hungry to pass her invitation up.

She tries and fails not to laugh at me as I put away two servings of leftover lasagna. "You can finish it off if you want," she says before she turns back to her book. I remember some sense of manners and leave the last two helpings for Jad.

After I wash my dishes, I can't sit down. I can't sit still. There's too much running around in my head. I keep seeing Claudia's damaged face, her torn up feet, her hands. The smell of gunpowder is still in my nose. I grab my camera and snap what I can from their back porch, though I don't think the forest service will use them. I check and I'm right. Another photog's images are up on my page already. Doesn't matter. Formatting these images will give me something else to burn in my mind. Something that isn't blood-soaked or bruised.

I spend the next three days up at the Tierneys'. I don't sleep for shit. Despite the fact that I saved Claudia from that son of bitch Smith, his body on my property seems to be fucking with everyone for one reason or another. Still, it's me who sees the hole I blew in his chest every time I close my eyes. I ignore the fact that the only rest

I've had for nearly half a week has been the few hours of shuteye I got with Claudia in that hospital bed.

The murders make the regional news. My mom leaves me a voicemail asking if I know anything about it, but I don't respond. Instead I'm reminded to call Evelyn and let her know that the Feds might check in on my whereabouts. She tells Meegan and Marcos what happened and they start blowing up my phone. Everyone at The Club is worried about me, but proud of me too. They've been following the news online. I stopped a monster. Milligan and Smith are monsters.

On the third day, May-Bell and I head to town to hit the market. I've eaten most of their food and she's worried cabin fever's getting the best of me. We take Titus with us. He needs a break too. Everyone I see has kind words and odd congratulations. Apparently Claudia's added to the myth of my greatness. Some people mention her by name. She feels indebted to me. It's not true, but there's no point in arguing. It'll just draw these conversations out.

When we stop by the diner to grab some pies May-Bell's ordered from Connie, Tanner and Lightfoot are enjoying a leisurely lunch at the counter when we walk in. Lightfoot greets me with a smile.

"Mr. Olsen," she says. "Just the man we were looking for." Everyone's quiet again, but it's different this time. They are ready for the suits to beat it. The case is closed as far as we're all concerned. One died and one's behind bars. There's not much left to sort out.

"Come on down here and pay, sweetheart," Connie says to May-Bell. "How you doing, Shep?"

"Just fine, Connie," I say before I turn to Lightfoot. "What can I do for you?"

"Nothing at all. We're heading out today. Sheriff Bingham has your truck waiting for you down at the station and you are free to enter your home."

"Is there going to be a trial?" I ask.

"With this confession and what we were able to collect, I don't expect there will be. But you never know. Even the red handed turn tail and try to save their own asses," Lightfoot says with a shrug.

Tanner waves at Connie and asks for the check. She doesn't acknowledge him, but drops the bill in front of his plate a few moments later anyway. He smirks then pulls out his wallet. "I'll need a receipt."

"Sure thing," she says, tight lipped.

"Thank you for your cooperation. We'll be in touch if we need anything else." Tanner collects his change and they leave.

"Do you mind if we drive by the hospital?" I ask May-Bell as we leave the diner. I take the warm pies out of her hands.

"Not at all," May-Bell says. She drops me off. I tell her I'll be back up to their place to grab Titus as soon as I get my truck. She tells me there's no rush. I know we're welcome in their home for as long as I'd like.

I don't even make it past the waiting room before Sarah calls out my name. I turn and she's coming down the hall with a folded piece of paper in her hand.

"Hey." She's a little out of breath. "She's gone. Left a few hours ago, but she left this for you."

I'm processing as I take the note out her hand. Lightfoot and Tanner knew she was gone. They knew I was gonna beat feet over to see her. Giving me the green light even though they knew she was gone was their last fuck you. I blink and look up at Sarah. She's looking at the note, then she looks up at me.

"Why are you looking at me like that?" I ask.

"I'm just wondering what it is about you, but at the same time, I know."

"We can't go back, Sarah. You said it yourself. You can't change for me and I can't change for you." It's heavy talk for a hospital waiting room, but I need my sanity back. All of it.

"I know we can't, Shep. I'm just worried. As a friend."

"I'm fine."

She rolls her eyes, then practically slams her hands on her hips. "I know, Shep. You're always fine, but I don't think she is."

"Say it. All of it."

"I'm saying that just because you're well enough to walk out of here doesn't mean you're well enough to just pick right up where you left off. I'm just saying that when a patient asks me several times for a pen and paper to write a note to the person who saved her life, and she's in tears when she hands it to me that *she is not fine.*"

I don't say anything because there's nothing to say. I can't sleep and no one tried to kill me. Claudia lost a lot that night. Peace of mind is only one of them.

"I don't know what's in the note. Like I said, I didn't read it," Sarah says.

"But?"

"If she wants you to write back, reply, she needs something."

I nod. Again, there's nothing to say.

"I'll be around if you want to talk."

"Thanks."

Sarah touches my hand and then she turns and walks away. I take my time walking back to the station. I don't want to read the note. Not yet. I find Sally behind the counter. She's less spooked this time around. She has a smile for me and she has my keys.

My truck is behind the station and it's all fucked up. Every inch is covered in finger print dust. The doors, the fender, all over the interior, all over the dash. I might as well burn the thing before I try to clean it. I climb behind the wheel and contemplate heading back to the market to find something to clean all this shit up, but I don't want the attention driving my bright blue piece of evidence through the center of town. The cleaning supplies up at my place will have to do. I climb behind the wheel. I unfold the note.

Shep, Sorry for the chicken scratch. My hand is still screwed up. I just wanted to say thank you. I asked if you were coming back because I wanted to thank you again in person and I wanted to say goodbye in person too, but they were pretty insistent about us not seeing each other until they wrapped up the investigation. I doubt I'll see you again. Clown or no clowns, I'm never leaving the comfort of the city again.

I thought losing my parents was the worst thing that could happen, but this was much worse. I wouldn't even be here to write this note if it wasn't for you. I'm going home. I'm going to pretend work is the perfect distraction until they release my brother's body and let me lay him to rest.

I keep telling myself there are people to blame for this and I am not one of those people, but I think it might take the rest of my life for that to really sink in. I'll save that for my grief counselor or therapist. Whoever you talk to after these things happen. I did think of another way this could have been worse. The scenario involves you not being home that night. And also, you could have missed twice. Anyway. Thank you, a hundred thousand times.

Love always, and I mean always. I'm naming a child or a really cute dog after you.

Claudia

P.S. Tanner and Lightfoot are dicks. I hope they didn't give you too hard of a time.

I scan the piece of paper again. Read it three and four more times. Her number doesn't magically appear. There isn't an email address or a website. No breadcrumbs to her cottage in the woods. Or her loft in the city. Sarah is right about a lot of things when it comes to me, but she doesn't know Claudia Cade. She is a fighter. She doesn't need me at all. She will be just fine.

CHAPTER FOUR

CLAUDIA

Week One

I realize I've been sitting on the edge of my couch staring at the fire escape for at least an hour when Liz comes through my apartment door. I know I look like shit. My head, my hand, and my foot are still bandaged up. My eye is less swollen, but it's still bruised as hell. My bosses at Kleinman's have given me an extended leave. Purchasing women's apparel for a major chain requires a lot of travel and a lot of face to face. They don't want me to scare away potential vendors with my mangled skin and broken body, but none of that matters. I can't bring myself to leave my small loft.

Liz is busy with her own life, but she is the first person I have the hospital contact. Hers is the only number I save in the stupid burner phone the Feds gave me a few days after they casually mention that everything from our campsite is to be used as evidence. Including my phone. And my brother.

Liz is all I have left.

I'm grateful, but I hope nothing makes it so I have to pay her back. Not like this.

"Hey pretty girl," she says in her usual bright cheery way. I blink a few times, focus on her face. "I have your favorite. Jerk chicken from Miss Rica."

"Thank you," I manage to say. My throat is perpetually raw these days.

"And I have your mail. This was outside." She holds up a small brown box from Amazon.

"That should be my phone."

"Oh good." She sets the food on the coffee table and hands me the box before she starts to peel off her trench coat.

"Thank you."

"No problem. There are drinks in the fridge from last night. I'll grab us those," she says. "What else can I get you?"

"A time machine." I had no idea tears can just leak out of your eyes like this, but since I got home I've almost stopped wiping my face. There's no point. I can't stop crying.

"Oh honey." I realize Liz is looking at me. I'm staring at the gold heart necklace hanging on her chest, the one I got her from work. She turns and heads for the kitchen. I turn back toward the TV. It's still off. I can't remember what I was planning to watch.

"Here." Liz hands me a paper towel, just barely dampened with water.

"Thank you." I wipe my eyes and my raw cheeks. I try to breathe normally. I can't, but the coolness of the paper towel makes my face feel better.

"I'm going to stay for a while," she says as she sits and starts distributing the chicken and rice.

"You don't have to." Liz has a real job, corporate litigation. I know her free time is precious.

"But I want to," she says. "Plus, we have at least two seasons of the Great French Baking Competition to watch."

I don't argue because I don't really want to be alone. I grab my blanket out of the corner of the couch. I wrap myself up while she finishes with the food and grabs the drinks. My hand throbs like crazy, but I manage to grip the remotes and find Liz's favorite baking competition show.

"Ooh, it's Tarts and Pies week. This is gonna be good." She flashes me a bright smile. I try to smile back, but mostly I just slow blink and think about how tired my eyes are.

I force some food down, listen to Liz's comments on whose crusts look the best in her opinion. She gets a text.

"It's Brooklyn."

"How is she?" I ask. I have a soft spot for her little sister.

"Still wild," she says with a smirk.

"You're still jealous."

"Of course I am," she laughs. "I should be worried that her flighty ass isn't going to pass the bar, but of course she is."

"The kid's just smart. She can't help it."

"She's like the anti-Elle Woods. No effort, all results. She says 'tell Claudia I say feel better and I love her.'"

My chest tightens and another huge tear comes. My blanket works just fine as a tissue this time. "Tell her the same," I say around the lump in my throat.

Liz puts down her phone and picks up the brown box on the table. "You want me to open this?"

I stare for a moment. "Yeah. It's been nice not having a phone for a while though."

"I'm sure."

I watch this poor woman burn the fuck out of a pie crust as Liz asks me the appropriate questions so she can activate my phone. By the time everything is finished backing up, we've moved on to the bread portion of the competition.

"Yikes," Liz says under her breath.

"What?"

"Just a lot of alerts. I'm guessing you haven't been checking your computer either."

"No. I told Lara to call me on the burner if it was important," I say. "And I can't really say anything until the Feds complete their investigation." I might be making that up. Maybe not. It's a good enough excuse.

"Okay. Let's see. We'll ignore the emails for now. Tons of text. Most of them are from Jason. Um yeah…He texted like ten minutes ago. Do you want me to respond to him?"

Liz and Jason aren't close. For the first time I'm grateful for that. She tolerates him for me, and just barely. When I left the hospital the nurse who checked me out told me only to take on as much as I can handle. Step one is stop crying. Step two will be facing people who will ask me an endless stream of questions. People like my boyfriend.

"Let me see." I hold out my bandaged hand and take my new phone. Those red dots with numbers in the double and triple digits cover the screen. I'm not checking

Facebook. Liz posted something for me and Miles's best friend, Owen, is handling things with their medical school friends.

There are so many voicemails, but I can't listen. I look at the texts. The previews are all the same, a hundred different versions of *I just heard. OMG, Are you okay? So sorry to hear about Miles.* I look at the texts from Jason. His are the most recent, and really, the most urgent.

I ran into Brooklyn.
She said you're back.
Are you back?
Why didn't you call me?

Something in my stomach sinks. It feels like acceptance. I can't hide from everyone, even if I want to. Still my gut is telling me to lie. I can't deal with any level of his shit right now.

I just got back this morning.
The cops still have all my stuff.
Including my phone.

Fuck. I'm coming over.

I want to tell him to stay home. Or stay at the office. Or just tell him to go to one of his usual haunts with his buddies because I'm sure the Mets are playing. He doesn't need to see me like this. I don't need to answer his questions. He's never even met Miles. And I *am* fine. I'm here. I'm alive. There's nothing to talk about. Suddenly

I'm nauseous and my chest hurts in a different way than it's been hurting for the last thirteen days.

I text *okay.*

I silence all my alerts and put my phone on the coffee table. I shove more chicken in my mouth. My throat's so dry I have to drink something before I choke. Still, the food helps.

"You okay?" Liz asks. She's carefully looking at my face and then she looks at my hands. I feel like I'm shaking, but I'm not.

"Just hungry. I should have eaten earlier."

She smiles and pats my knee. "Get those nutrients in, boo boo."

I finish my dinner. I have more water. A sweet South Asian man with no hair and thick glasses wins the bread challenge. The youngest contestant, a mousy white girl who definitely had some skills is sent home. Next up is cakes. I wait.

My heart freezes when the buzzer goes off.

"You expecting anyone?" Liz asks, confused.

"I'm pretty sure that's Jason."

She stands and starts for the door. "I'll buzz him in...if you want."

"Yeah. Of course."

She makes her way over to the intercom and hits the button. "Hey, it's Liz. Come on up."

"Thanks." I can hear it in his voice. He's pissed. Instantly I think of the man who saved me. I think of Shep Olsen. Every time I think of Jason, I think of Shep. I'm not sure why. But I count the seconds I know it'll take Jason to ride the elevator up to my floor and I think of

Shep sitting next to my bed. I think about his fingers touching mine.

Liz flicks the locks and starts cleaning up the remains of our dinner. She knows what comes next.

Jason opens the door. I turn around, but I don't get up. Liz is already sliding on her jacket.

"Claudia," he says in a way that instantly makes me regret answering his text. I know what I look like. Step one: stop crying. Step two: heal so people stop looking at you the way Jason is currently looking at me.

Liz sighs. She's pissed. "I'm going to head home. Do you need anything else?"

"No, I'm fi—"

"I got it from here," Jason interrupts. Lawyers, always with the pissing contests.

"I'm fine," I say again. I stand and hobble a couple inches, ignoring the way Jason's looking at my hands and my feet. Liz meets me more than halfway and hugs me.

"Just call me if you need me, okay? I'll come right back over."

"I will."

There's a terse "see you later" with Jason and then she's gone. Some of the tension drains out of the room. It's always like this. The molecules in the air can only handle so much posturing at once. Jason comes around the couch. His blue eyes are still hard on me. He's still pissed.

"Why didn't you call me?"

"I just got a phone. Today. The cops have my other one in an evidence bag somewhere."

"Was your computer stolen too?" he snaps. Usually I'd tell him to fuck off. This time I'm quiet. I flinch.

He's quiet for a moment before he sighs. "I'm sorry. I'm just stressed out from work. And I was worried about you. And Miles," he tacks on.

You didn't even know Miles, I almost say. I just swallow instead. "I'm glad you're here, but I don't really want to talk about it right now."

"No, I get it. You've been through a lot. I mean, look at you. You look like you went toe to toe with a bear."

"Close." His voice flashes in my ears. That sick laugh. He's telling me to keep running. It's funny to him. It's a game. He's going to catch me.

"I know just what you need. Sit," Jason says.

I sit. He grabs the remotes and finds the Mets game. Once he's situated with a glass of whiskey from the bottle he keeps above my fridge, he pulls me into his arms and tugs the blanket over me. I try to breathe.

"I know baseball always knocks you out. Just let the sweet sounds of the third inning rock you to sleep."

Typically this is where I laugh, where I sarcastically thank him for being so considerate, then leave him to the game while I catch up on work emails or playfully tease his cock through his pants until he's forced to momentarily abandon the game to get me off. Tonight I just swallow and settle against his chest. There are more silent tears. He absently asks me if I'm okay, but he's screaming at the second baseman before I can answer.

I stare at the fire escape. Eventually I fall asleep.

*

Month Four

They don't tell you how long it can take to release a body. Or how long a federal prosecutor will take to tell you things you already know. Like how there won't be a trial because your brother's killer confessed and they need to extradite him to another state to stand trial for a triple murder he won't cop to. The bureaucracy doesn't give a shit about your feelings.

I get Miles back though. What's left of him. It makes more sense to bury him on the West coast. He went to college and med school in California. All his friends are there. Liz and Owen are now fast friends. Between the two of them, they inform all the people who need to be informed. Help me settle things with Miles's apartment and his car. They find a time and a place for his memorial service. Liz does her best, but eventually I have to talk to some of the people who miss Miles, who counted on him being around. They need me to assist with their closure.

There are awful conversations with a woman named Preeti. I have no idea who the fuck she is, but she gets my number from Liz on Facebook and she takes it personally that my brother never mentioned her to me. I'm a dick for telling her that, even though I don't say it in such harsh terms. Preeti is his girlfriend. She thinks they were going to get married. I don't refute that 'cause I realize that I have no way of knowing if that was true or not.

When she meets Liz and I at the Paluma County morgue, I tell her I'm sure he misses her, whatever the fuck that even means. He's dead. I apologize for being short on the phone. I tell her I'm sorry that Miles wasn't the one to properly introduce us. I tell her I'm sorry in general. I am. She cries all over me in the parking lot, until Liz suggest we go inside. I throw up when I finally view Miles's body. I don't even try to contain myself. You're not prepared for something like a pep talk from the county's sweetest coroner. "This is going to be difficult" does not cover it. They know it's going to be so difficult that they have a wastebasket at the ready.

My brother is gone. After weeks and weeks of being told to be patient. I can't even do the weird things I've been dreaming of like squeezing his hand one more time or kissing his forehead and telling him I'm comforted by the fact that he's with our parents again. I'm not looking at my brother. I'm looking at a slashed and gutted husk sutured back together again, a grotesque monster movie version of what my brother used to be. The pain rises in my chest again. The crashing is back in my ears. I can hear his screams, mixing with the sounds of the brush crunching under my feet. The sounds of that man chasing me. I've tried to cope without my brother these last few months, but when I see him, we are back in those woods again.

Shep pops into my mind. I fight the image of him back.

Preeti loses it, crumples on the floor in a sobbing heap. I find strange comfort in comforting her. Her shaking gives me something to focus on. Liz asks again what the cost of cremation will be. I don't argue when Preeti tells me there's this place in Santa Cruz where she'd like to spread Miles's ashes. I want to keep part of him with me, but letting him go all together feels like the right thing to do.

We leave Preeti at the hotel. All of us are too raw to even to talk about what we've just seen. I can't even form real sentences. I just keep thinking, *my poor, sweet brother. He didn't deserve this.* Those words, over and over, he didn't deserve this. And another simple phrase. I want Shep.

Liz continues to be a rockstar. She makes sure I'm hydrated and fed. We both know it's a forgone conclusion that I won't sleep well, but she climbs into the double bed on my side of the hotel room with me and she's still there at two in the morning when my body forces me to stop crying and sleep.

In the morning, I almost tell her about Shep. She knows he saved me, but she doesn't know the rest. That my brain is hopelessly grasping at the moments I spent with him in my hospital bed. Those were the last moments of normalcy I remember. The last time I remember laughing without feeling guilty. Those stupid clowns. Quinten isn't too far from Stanford, not that far. Less than a half day's drive. I could see him. I'm contemplating how to plausibly show up in Shep's town with no explanation when Jason texts me and tells me he's boarding his flight.

That night Preeti cancels our dinner plans. She's saving up her energy for the service. Liz begs off for dinner too. I don't even ask if she's sure. She's exhausted and even though she didn't know Miles well, I know she cares about me enough that this whole awful situation is weighing heavily on her. It's been clear the last few months that she can take care of me or pretend to tolerate Jason, but not both. I feel awful and thank her for the millionth time for being the amazing way she is.

After he checks in and moves my stuff to his room, I listen to Jason talk about his clients as he finishes off his third beer in the hotel restaurant. I want to choke him, but it helps distract me. I need to put my own feelings aside. If Jason can forget that he's in town for a funeral, surely I can too. The distraction works until we climb into bed and he tries to slide his hand between my legs. I tell him I'm not in the mood. He comments that I haven't been in the mood for months.

He apologizes when he realizes that I am not against stabbing him with the blue hotel pen on the night stand. It just hasn't been months. That's a full blown lie. I fucked his brains out two days before I left the city. He apologizes again. He's just worried, he says. I haven't been myself. He hopes the funeral will give me what I need. I scream at him, tell him how he has no idea what this feels like. I tell him he's being selfish. When I calm down I'm so pissed at him that I don't have any nightmares.

The next morning, when we get to the church, I take on the role of silent mourner, and people seem to be completely okay with that. The service is for Miles and his friends. I'm still here. I survived. I'll see my friends again, hold Jason, fuck him again. Preeti cries enough for the both of us.

As we walk to the reception, Jason slides his hand around my waist. I try to forget the fight we had the night before. I think of Shep's fingers brushing mine.

Month Six

"I'm thinking about quitting my job," I say to my therapist. It's been suggested to me a few times that I see someone. My boss Lara insists upon it after I tell overrated modeling phenom Kaitey Taylor to shut the fuck up as we both head to the lobby of the Kleinman's building. I'm not "handling" my grief and my temper seems to be "spiraling."

"You seem to need a cleansing of sorts. You said that you separated from your boyfriend last week and now you want to leave your job," my therapist says.

"I just don't trust myself to keep my job right now."

"And why do you think that is?"

I like Dr. Mao, but I hate talking to her. I have no idea how you're expected to tell your therapist the truth. I barely tell myself the truth.

"I'm not happy."

"Are you not happy with the job or are you not happy with your employer?"

"I'm not sure." Another lie.

"How have you been sleeping?"

"About the same."

"Not very much then."

"Not consistently," I say.

"Have you been keeping up with your sleep journal?"

"No, but either I can't sleep or I want to sleep all the time. Or I'm waking up at weird hours."

"Are you still having nightmares?"

My throat closes. "No."

"There is nothing that dictates that you need to keep working there, but I would recommend contemplating next steps before making a hasty exit."

I nod and turn my phone over in my lap. It's off, but fidgeting with it is better than looking at my hands when they're empty. Some of the scars will fade, but a lot of the deep cuts will leave their tracks in my skin forever.

"I don't want to go back," I say.

"Can you tell me why?

"I just don't want to be there." I'm not sure I want to be in the city, I almost add.

"Well you haven't had a real break since your brother's funeral, from what you've told me. A break or a fresh start might be a good idea."

"Yeah."

"Have you needed to use the breathing exercises this week?"

Like seventeen times a day. "No. I tried to tune people out."

She scribbles something down. I almost close my eyes and take a deep breath and count to ten. Almost.

CHAPTER FIVE

SHEP

"Climate change isn't real, my ass," I say to no one, but Titus is looking up at me when I glance over at him. The sun is finally breaking through the clouds, giving me a chance at the shot I've been wanting for the last few days. This time of year the mountain typically has a few inches of snow, but it's too warm. All we're getting is rain.

I shoot for a while, catching the sun as it breaks through the clouds in the distance and passes under the horizon. I give Titus his moments of vanity and take a few shots of him exploring the underbrush and rocks that surround the paths on the way back to my place. It's full dark before we break through onto my property and the temperature has dropped, but I'm in no rush.

I put my gun away, then set my camera bag and my walkie down, and go to grab Titus his dinner. I see the notification light is blinking on my house phone. It's enough to sidetrack me. No one ever calls that number unless they need me down the mountain and they can't get me on my cell. I go to hit the button and my phone rings again. The noise is so loud and grating I snatch it off the cradle before it can ring another time.

"Hello?"

"You busy?" It's Connie. I can hear Paul shouting out orders in the background.

"Not really. Something the matter?"

"That girl, Claudia Cade. She's in town. She came by the diner asking for you."

"What?" I'm not sure I heard her right.

"That girl you saved. The one you brought down the mountain. She was just here. Jerry was in when she first came in. He was shocked to see her, but as soon as he left she asked me if I knew where to find you."

I'm silent for a few moments too long. I hear Connie, but it's not making any sense.

"Shep."

"She still there?" I ask.

"No. I had her hang tight and gave her something to eat while I tried to get a hold of you. She just left."

"Did she say where she was going?"

"She mumbled something about the hospital. She might have gone over there. You want me to call and see if Fern's checked in yet?"

"No, no. You don't have to. I'll come down and see if I can find her. Thanks, Connie."

"Not a problem."

I ignore the way my heart is suddenly pounding and set down the phone. I have to feed Titus, I tell myself, and I have to put my gear away. Once that's taken care of I do my damnedest not to drive off the road as I race my truck down to the bottom of the mountain.

The hospital's a bust. One of the nurses I'm not familiar with tells me that Claudia's been by the QER and dropped off some flowers for Fern. She's said she'll be back in the morning to see Sarah and the other girls on the day shift. If she's still in town I know there are only two places she could be staying.

My short search brings me to the row of green and grey semi-attached cabins just off the highway. I pull into the Light Grass Lodges. There are only a few cars out front. The bell rings loudly when I open the front door, but Kaleb McCray is already at the desk.

"Hey man," he says, stretching out his hand. I haven't seen him in a while, but we try to catch up over at the bar every now and then. We clap palms and he reaches over the counter to pat me on the back. "What brings you over here?"

"Do you have a guest staying here? Name's Claudia Cade. I checked over at The Mountain View, but Sam said they were all booked up."

"Oh! Yeah. I—hold on. We're not supposed to give out guests' room numbers."

"She's here though, right?"

"Yeah she just stopped in and asked for extra towels. When I brought them to her it looked like she was settling in for the night."

"Uh, yeah if you could call her room and tell her I'm here, that would be cool."

"Not a problem, man." He reaches for the phone. "I shouldn't be surprised you're here to see her. Haven't seen a chick that hot around here in years. Of course Shepard Olsen the First has already laid claim to her."

I don't respond. He doesn't need to know that I have no idea what she looks like when she's not covered in blood or bruises or bandages.

"Miss Cade?" he says, his voice suddenly professional. "Hi, It's Kaleb at the front desk. I have a Mr. Shep Olsen here to see you." He pauses for a moment. "Would you like me to give him your room number?" Another pause. "Absolutely. I will let him know. Absolutely. You are very welcome." He hangs up. The persona drops. "She's coming up here. She said give her a few minutes."

"Thanks."

"So how do you know this chick?"

I turn around and look at the picture of Kaleb's grandparents mounted on the wall by the light switches. "Kind of a long story."

"She had a New York ID. Must be a good story if she came all the way out here to see you."

"It's not. The double murders back in April. That's how we met."

"Holy shit. That's her?" The chatter around the county about Claudia and her brother, the man I'd killed and the scumbag that survived his run-in with Will's cruiser didn't die down until late summer, but I was sure everyone had heard an approximation of the events.

"Yeah. That's her. Maybe relax a little when she comes in here."

"Yeah, yeah. Of course. Sorry. That's some heavy shit."

"Yeah."

Kaleb defaults to football and starts telling me about how he's trying to get time off to use the Seahawks tickets his uncle got him for his birthday. We're talking about the Rams' move when I hear the front door click and the bell ring a half second later. I turn around and Claudia is standing there. She looks different than I remember, but I know it's her. At the time, I was more concerned with her living through the night than I was with her looks, but Kaleb wasn't wrong. She's hot as fuck.

She's shorter than me, like most everyone in a hundred mile radius, but she's not very short. She's wearing tight dark pants, some high tan boots, and one of those puffer winter jackets with a fur lined hood that somehow manages to hug her tits and her waist. She has makeup on, but she doesn't need it. Her hazel eyes and her lips speak for themselves. She's carrying a bouquet of roses. She smiles at me.

"Hi," she says. That's her voice, my brain tells me. I've only heard it a handful of times, but it's burned into my memory along with other things from that night.

"Hey."

She stands just inside the door for a moment before she snaps me out of whatever trance I'm still in and walks right up to me. She's just inches from me when she hands me the flowers. "These are for you. Pink is for gratitude."

I take them. "You didn't have to."

"I did."

We're both silent again. I can feel Kaleb watching us. Claudia glances past my shoulder as if to confirm that fact. She looks back up at me. The smile has faded. I don't think either of us have thought much beyond this moment. She was looking for me. I found her. Now what?

"There are services that deliver these things, I've heard," I say sarcastically, nodding at the flowers.

She smiles again. "I've heard, but I needed to do this."

I don't argue. Instead I nod in understanding. I get it. There have been things I've needed to do too.

"I—are you busy? I mean, do you have plans tonight?" she asks.

"No. You want to get out of here?"

"Yeah, actually. Is there somewhere we can talk?"

"Yeah. I can drive."

"Okay."

"Come on." I lightly take her arm. I almost pull away as she falls into step beside me, but I don't. Instead my hand slides to the small of her back as I open the door for her.

I flip Kaleb the finger as the door closes behind me.

The sound of the bell mixes with his laugh.

The Peak is full with its usual Thursday night football crowd. And by full, I mean four of the regulars are crowded around the bar, grumbling at the old mounted TV. I greet the boys and ignore the double and triple takes they all shoot in Claudia's direction. I tap on the counter and tell Rich to send two beers back to our table. Then I lead Claudia to a booth in the back of the worn-down watering hole. I watch her as she strips off her coat and almost choke. The shirt she's wearing is a simple black tee, but it's low cut and her tits are almost spilling out. They look so good, even if she were mine I wouldn't tell her to cover up.

"I didn't order for you out of some weird misogynistic shit. Blue Moon is the fanciest thing they have here."

She smiles again as she scans my face. "It's okay. A beer will loosen me up. Now that I'm looking at you I can see how crazy this is."

"What, you being here in Quinten?"

"Yeah. I told myself I thought this through, but thinking and doing are different things."

I feel the nervous energy rolling off her, but she keeps her eyes on my face. She's cataloging my features. She's not the only one. I want to reach across the table to see if the golden brown skin that covers the expanse from her forearm to her elbow is as soft as it looks.

"I don't think it's crazy." Crazy is the amount of time I've spent thinking about her in the last several months. "I wouldn't have come down here if I was bothered by you being here."

"Someone narced on me, huh?" Another smile. Fuck, her lips.

"See those guys at the bar and the bartender? Known them all since I was five years old. Kaleb back at the Lodges? He's my drinking buddy, when I come down to drink. It's a small town. Someone is always narcing on you."

"That must be weird." She sighs and plucks a napkin out of the holder. "I still shouldn't have shown up like this and I cannot even pretend that I just happened to be driving by."

"I'm sorry about back at the motel. You don't—" I stop myself from saying what almost comes out of my mouth.

"I don't have to explain why I flew three thousand miles to give you thank-you flowers?"

I shake my head. "I think there's something to be said about boundaries, but I don't think you showing up is out of bounds. I wanted to see you again."

"You did?"

"I tried to come right back to the hospital, and the feds wouldn't let me. They told me to stay away from you until their investigation was done. And then you were gone."

Her face goes blank.

"They didn't tell you," I say.

"No. They—the cops and the staff at the hospital were pretty insistent about me resting and healing enough to travel and then they were discharging me. An agent picked me up and drove me straight to the airport."

"They seemed to have an unnecessary flair for the dramatic. I got your note."

Rich comes over before she can respond and hands us our beers. He stares a moment too long at Claudia when she thanks him.

"Uh, yeah. I wrote that note in sort of a panic. They weren't—they didn't handle things very well."

"We don't have to talk about it," I say. She's stops looking at me and starts to frantically destroy the label on her bottle of beer.

"Do you have nightmares?" she asks.

"Yes," I answer.

She looks up at me. "I quit my job. And I dumped my boyfriend."

"Because of the nightmares?"

"Because neither was making me feel better when I was awake."

"What do you do, for work?" I ask. This is something I've wondered for a while. One of the many things I wondered about her.

"I was a buyer for Kleinman's flagship store. What do you do?"

"I'm a photographer for the forest service and I do some digital design work."

She says nothing again at first. She's going to town on that label. Someone scores and there's a bit of commotion to fill the silence. I wait.

"What do you have nightmares about?" she asks.

"Shit that makes me think I should probably talk to a shrink."

"But?"

"But I know I won't."

"I saw a shrink."

"How did that work out?"

"Dumped her too. And now I'm here." Claudia takes a long swig of her beer. She avoids my eyes, but she's still very pointedly looking at my chest.

"I was worried about you, but then I realized it was more like I was worried about my own psyche if I didn't get some kind of closure about this whole shit," I tell her.

"What kind of closure did you need?"

You. Seeing you, touching you, claiming you in a very specific way, I want to say, but I can't. I know the tricks my mind is playing on me. The months of thinking about her molded her into someone I know she isn't. A figment of my imagination. If I can just dominate that person one time, the person in my mind, bring her to the peak, break her and bring her back down safely I know we'll both exorcise the demons that keep me up at night. That keep me from setting foot in the woods on the east side of my property.

"Just to know I did the right thing."

"You did," she says.

I feel my jaw tensing. *You're a good boy*, I hear my grandfather say. *Too good. You've got to stick up for yourself.*

"I know," I say. "Seeing you helps."

"Does it?"

"Yes."

"Seeing you helps me too. I don't remember you being this tall."

"I don't remember you being this sexy," I say truthfully.

A hint of red crawls across her skin and she takes another sip of her beer. Then she clears her throat. "Don't say stuff like that."

"I apologize. I won't do it again."

"I just wanted to see you, but we're practically strangers still. I don't think fucking you would be a good idea. You...nevermind. I can't say that."

"Can't say what?" I push.

"I can't make a certain comparison. You and I don't have a before."

"What do you mean?"

"You didn't know me before."

"Have you changed?"

"Yes and no, but enough about me. Tell me about this gorgeous little mountain town. I thought it would be weird to be back, but it's been okay. Everyone is so nice it's distracted me from any mounting anxiety."

I almost laugh at the thought of Kaleb's customer service voice and how Rich typically would have told me I could pick up my own damn beers at the bar.

"It's pretty much what you get is what you see. Permanent number of residents is pretty small. There are seasonal folks that come in the spring and the summer, but we all know each other pretty well for the most part."

"And you have family here?"

"No."

"Oh."

"It was me and my grandfather until he passed away about five years back," I explain.

"So you're an orphan like me."

"Not exactly. My parents are still alive. They split their time between Colorado and D.C."

"Oh."

"My father is a blue blood senator from Colorado, been in the public eye his whole life. My mom was his mistress. When his wife died, my mom dropped me here with my grandfather so she could marry him."

Her mouth is sort of hanging open.

"Without this," I scrub my beard with my fingers, "he and I could be twins. It wouldn't make sense if his new girlfriend already had a five year old that looked exactly like him. He thought it was better if I didn't exist."

"Oh. Wow. Yeah. My whole family's just dead."

"I think both are pretty fucked up."

"True."

I finally take a sip of my beer and decide it's best if we keep the conversation focused on her. I can't say anything else that won't scare her off.

"Not sure this makes sense considering what you've already told me, but are you okay?"

"Little of column A, little of column B."

I sit back. The alternative involves taking her hand.

"The therapy helped with the survivor's guilt. So in that respect I just really miss my brother." A single huge tear rolls out of her eye and then another, but her voice doesn't waver. She grabs some napkins and wipes her cheeks. "Sometimes I even feel good about being alive. Like I don't wish I was dead, I just wish he was here with me."

"That makes sense. What's going on with column B?"

She sighs and sits back too. "It involves being angry pretty much all the time."

"Ah. I can see that."

"Yeah?"

I lean forward and show her the healed cuts on my knuckles. "Punched a tree a few months back."

She leans forward and runs her fingers over my hand. I ignore the heat and focus on the noticeable scars that cover her own skin.

"I was walking with a limp for so long that I thought I'd done permanent damage to my hip," she says.

"How's the hip now?"

"Fine. But sometimes when I have a shitty dream and I wake up, I fall back into the limp for a few minutes." She laughs, then chugs the rest of her beer. "I feel like we're Army buddies sharing our old war stories."

She's not wrong. A lot happened that night and neither of us have recovered from it. "Tell me what you need," I say.

She shakes her head and then tips the bottle back to claim the last few drops. "I can't."

"Why not?"

"Because it's delusional and selfish. So I settled for flowers. I wanted to thank you and the nurses who took care of me. And even Sheriff Bingham who actually tried to keep me informed."

"Tell me what you need," I say again.

"I can't."

I give up and move on. Pressuring her is useless. And a dick move. "When do you head home?"

She shrugs. "Whenever I want, I guess. I planned to see my brother's girlfriend in San Francisco before I head back, but ya know. No job, no rush."

And no boyfriend to get back to, I think.

"I don't know. I want to get to know you better," she says. "I want us to be close."

"I think we are close."

"But it's weird. I don't know you."

I nod. Clearly I'm not the only one struggling with this.

"I looked for you online. You're hard to find."

"I'm not on social media and my photography is under S. Olsen."

"Did you look for me?"

"No."

Pain flashes in her eyes for just a second.

"It was for the best, I think."

"I should go," she says suddenly. She stands and grabs her jacket. "Do you mind giving me a lift back?"

"Claudia."

"Really. I just wanted to see you and say thank you. I'm not sure if you're a vase guy or even a flower guy, but a mug or even a tall glass will work just fine if you cut down the stems enough."

I look at her for a few more seconds, but she's avoiding my eyes. She's done. I stand and grab her empty and what's left of my beer, then nod for her to lead the way. I ignore the look on Rich's face when I leave the empties and a twenty on the bar.

On the short ride back to the Lodges, Claudia looks out the window of my truck and comments on the quaintness of the town. I think of how there's no way I can salvage this night. There is nothing to salvage. It's all in my head. She points me to the car that's parked in front of her cabin and I pull up next to it. I get out and walk her to her door.

"Well, thank you for coming down to see me. I know it's weird, me being here," she says.

"It's not weird. Let me see your phone. I'm going to give you my numbers this time," I say. She peers up at me for a moment, but then she reaches into her pocket and pulls out her cellphone. She hands it to me. I type in my cell and my house phone numbers, label them appropriately. I give her back her phone.

"Call me before you leave."

"I will." She bites her lip, then looks at the part in the curtains that cover the cabin window. I watch as the orange glow from the porch light plays across her face. She looks back up at me. "It was nice to see you, Shep. I owe you my life."

"You don't owe me anything."

She huffs out a little laugh and looks down. She swallows. She closes her eyes for a moment and then she looks back up at me and holds out her hand. "Mr. Olsen."

I pull her into my arms and kiss the top of her head. "Keep stretching out that hip," I say. She sags against me and that's when my brain decides it's time to go. I grip her shoulders and stand away. I see the hurt play across her face again. I have to go. There's no see ya. No goodbye. I turn and get in my truck. And leave.

I'm almost at the pass when my phone rings. It's a 718 number. I slow down and pull over to the side of the road.

"Hello?"

"Why didn't you look for me?" She's crying. "I could have died in your arms and then I vanish with this note that frankly reads like something my mom would have forced me to write to thank a tutor for their time and you don't look for me?"

"Because."

"Because why? Tell me. I didn't imagine what happened in the hospital and I'm not saying it was anything sexual. And I appreciate that you came to check on me at all, but you didn't have to stay with me. You didn't have to hold me the way you did. How was it so easy for you to walk away after you got my note?"

I feel my forehead start to throb. "Don't do that."

"Do what?"

"Pretend like that note had your address and phone number at the bottom and I was just too cold hearted to use them. That letter felt like a thank you and farewell to me. You had returned to your old life. Tell me where the line is between concern and stalking."

She's quiet for a while before she responds, but I know she's still there.

"I'm sorry." She lets out a watery breathe. "I'm sorry. I—I told you what I needed was selfish and delusional."

"What would have happened if I just showed up in New York three months ago? Would you have been okay with that? Would your boyfriend have been okay with that?" It's low, but it's the truth.

"I know. I just—it hurts. You said you thought about me. Weren't you the least bit curious?"

"Claudia."

"Just tell me please. Maybe I just need to hear what's actually going through your head. Maybe that'll actually help more than giving you roses."

I close my eyes and clench my free hand. My cock is already rising as I consider what I actually want.

"Shep."

"Curious doesn't cover it," I say. "Seeing you that hurt, it gutted me. I wanted to protect you and take care of you, but I knew that wasn't—"

"It wasn't what?"

"It was all about me. It was what *I* wanted and what *I* needed. I couldn't put that on you."

"Can you come back to the motel? Please?"

I know I shouldn't. "Why?" I ask.

"Because I didn't come here to see you for five minutes. I can admit that."

"Why did you come here?"

"I don't know." She almost shouts. This is the part I didn't want to deal with because it's not cut and dried. It's a fucking mess. But I can't walk away from her.

"I can't stay. I left my dog up at my place."

"Then let me come up."

"Are you sure?"

"Yes."

"A lot happened up at my place, Claudia. I'm bringing you right back down if you can't handle it."

"I'm not—" she stops herself. She brings herself back to reality. My house, my yard, it's a part of her war story. Neither of us know what demons she'll find up there. "Okay," she finally says.

I sigh. This isn't about me. It's about her. "Go to the front desk and wait for me."

"Why?"

"So we can tell Kaleb you're coming up to my place."

"Why does the hotel clerk need to know our business?"

"Because when beautiful women come into towns like this and leave their cars at roadside motels it's good for a few people to have an idea of what's going on and where they actually went."

"Oh. Okay, yeah. That's not a bad idea."

"I'll be right there." I end the call and make sure it's clear for me to make a u-turn.

I'm making a huge fucking mistake.

CHAPTER SIX

I take my time driving back up to my place, even when I hit the split to my private road. Claudia is quiet most of the time. She comments on the trees every now and then. I tell her it's greener than usual thanks to all the rain we've been getting. It's not raining now, but it's due to start up again soon I tell her. Sticking to the weather and the terrain seems to be safe. When we pull up to my gate, I realize I didn't close it when I left. I know why. I won't beat myself up about it.

I watch Claudia out of the corner of my eye as the security lights around my property pop on. I pull my truck to a stop in its usual spot. I wait a minute, gauge her reaction.

"This is your place?"

"Yeah."

She frowns. "I don't remember this."

"I'm not going to sit here and try to shock you into remembering."

"Good call. Let's go inside."

I cut the engine, grab the roses out of the back seat, then meet her around the passenger side. I'm tempted to take her hand when she hops out of the cab, but I don't. I don't know where we are, but it's not there.

"I remember this," she says when she steps up on the porch. She's looking at my front door.

"Are you okay?" I ask, but I don't pause as I raise my keys. We don't need to stand on my porch a second longer.

"I'm fine," she says. "But I remember."

I open the door and usher her inside. Titus's head pokes up from the couch. He lets out a pathetic half bark and runs over to greet us. Claudia steps half behind me. She drops the handle on her overnight bag.

"Is he friendly?"

"Very. Just hold out your hand," I say but Titus is already busy sniffing her thigh. She drops her fingers down and gives his head a tentative scratch.

"Hey boy." The scratch isn't enough. He wiggles his head under her fingers and when that isn't enough he sets about licking her whole hand.

I fight a smile and walk into the kitchen to find a blade and a mason jar for the flowers. "Make yourself at home," I say.

"This is a huge dog."

"Yeah. We call him the super mutt."

"Makes sense though. I couldn't see you with a small dog."

"It's not smart to have a pet that large birds can eat out here in the woods."

"Ah, yeah. That makes way more sense. Not much of a guard dog though, are you?"

I take out my butcher knife and cut off the bulk of the stems. When I turn around, after they are settled in their makeshift vase, Claudia is squatting on the floor rubbing Titus's face.

"You're just a giant baby, aren't you," she says in pseudo baby talk.

I stand there and look at them for a minute, until Claudia realizes I'm watching her. She stands and clears her throat. "I didn't think this through," she says.

"Do you want me to take you back down? I'll take you back."

"No," she says, like that's a ridiculous idea. She sighs and looks up at the beams above our heads. "I know I mentioned this in the bar, but I still don't know how to explain it without it sounding nuts."

"I think we're past that. How about you just be as honest with me as you can?"

"Deal. But it goes both ways."

I think for a second before I agree. I know whatever I have to say will definitely cut our night short, but a deal is a deal. "Fine."

"Your house is really nice."

"I remodeled the whole interior with my neighbor a few years ago. Did their place too."

Her eyebrows shoot up. "You have neighbors?"

"They aren't close. Maybe two miles away on the next rise. The road forks toward their place about halfway down the mountain."

"Oh. Well you guys did a nice job. Not that I have any clue what it looked like before." I head over to the mantle and grab the framed photo that's been there for as long as I can remember. I walk over to Claudia.

"This is me and my grandfather. He was showing me how to clean the fireplace." May-Bell had taken the picture while she was standing in the kitchen. She'd captured more of the great room in its original state.

"Cute kid."

I put the picture back in its place. I turn around and she's still standing by the door, still in her coat. "You were saying?"

"Right. Me and my mistakes. Do you ever feel like you're looking at two shitty options?"

"Before I answer, are we staying for a little while at least? I'd love to offer you a drink. Have a seat or something," I know my tone sounds dickish, but it's getting hard to stand around looking at her with so many different variables undecided.

"Yes. We're staying." Finally she takes off her coat and hangs it on the rack by the door. I ditch my own jacket on the back of the couch and walk into the kitchen.

"To answer your question, yes. About the shitty options. I've been there."

"Right and maybe one of those options is the sane, smart option, but it comes with huge what ifs that you know will eat at you, possibly for years to come."

"Yeah, I've been there before." I grab two glasses and the pitcher of water from the fridge and bring them over to the couch. She sits down at the other end, leaving Titus plenty of room to jump up between us and make himself comfortable.

"God, he's cuddly."

"You can use him as an excuse to change the subject a few more times, but eventually we should really talk about this."

"We're talking," she said with an offended laugh. "Anyway, Pushy. Okay. So one option, I stay home. I maybe find a new therapist. I definitely still dump my boyfriend, but I try to move on. I try to stop thinking of this hypothetical version of you I've created in my head based on the facts I was able to piece together after I suffered a head injury and a decent amount of blood loss. I heal?" She uses air quotes.

"What's option two?"

"I come here."

"And?"

"I tell you what's been going on."

"And you're going to do that?"

"I guess so. We did make a deal. Okay." She lets out a deep breath. "Option two is I come here and I tell you that I've been wanting to see you in this very specific, weird way. I think it's some sort of survivor's thing. I mean I know it is. But I don't know how you enter into any interpersonal relationship that way. Like this super fucked up thing happened and we were both there. Wanna be friends?"

"You could say that. I wouldn't think that was weird."

Her head rolls back on the couch cushion and she glares at me.

"How did you come to your decision? This feels like option two," I say.

"I tried option one for a couple months and it wasn't working."

"So you want to see if we can be friends? We can do that. What's the shitty side of that?"

"Also two-sided. I get here and you don't even live here anymore or you're like WTF bitch, leave me alone."

I smile a little. "Well that didn't happen."

"Right, but I haven't told you the part where I've been so fucked up that I think I've become obsessed with you. Things were so bad that sometimes I could only self comfort by thinking about you holding me."

I swallow and look down at Titus with his head resting in Claudia's lap. "Did you come out here because you want me to hold you?"

She sighs, loud, and runs her hand through her hair. I realize then that her bangs are covering up the massive scar that cuts close to her hair line. "Yes and no. Yes because yes, but no because I'm really afraid that something inside me is so...broken that I'll never be able to function again if you're not holding me."

I nod. I understand. "Dependency."

"Exactly. So seeing you, since you seem to be okay with that part, is fine. But then what happens? Did punching a tree help you? Maybe I should try that."

"It helped for a little while."

"Well what's your plan? How does Shep move past this?"

I pause for a moment. "I'll...preface this with a disclaimer. I'm not trying to shock you and I'm not trying to sound cocky and I don't want you to think that I'm trying to talk down to you or impress you."

She frowns and tilts her head a bit to the side. "Okay."

"I have a coping mechanism and it is sexual—"

"You let a dominatrix put out cigarettes on your chest?" she says, a sarcastic smile flashing across her lips.

"No, but I do belong to a bondage club in Los Angeles. I usually go there once a year, but I was thinking about going more than once, or earlier than usual. I needed to expend this energy in a certain way. I need to be with a submissive for a longer session. I'm pretty sure that would do the trick. Though I've never been involved in a murder investigation before so..."

"Right. There's a first time for everything. So are you telling me you have scheduled sex once a year?"

"I have scheduled sex once a year for a week straight, but yes."

Her eyes flash wide before she turns her attention back to the spot behind Titus's ear. "Hmmm. Casual kink is a preference of mine, but I've never set foot in a club. Are you the Dominant or the submissive?"

"A Dominant."

Another hmmm. "I'm trying to paint this fuller picture of you in my head. Do you only *want* to have sex once a year?"

"No, but this is a small town."

"Ah slim pickings."

"Possibly."

"You're not sure?"

"I've only had one relationship with someone local. After that I didn't exactly hold interviews for a replacement. So far my system has been working."

"Until I came along."

"You know it isn't like that."

"I know. I— yeah. So I want to be held and you want to dominate your submissive."

"That's not what I said," I snap.

Claudia's brows pull together as she frowns at me. "Sorry. I think I heard you wrong."

"I didn't mean to be short. I apologize." I consider taking back our deal and taking her back down the mountain. "I don't have a submissive. Not one that belongs to me. I have an arrangement with a submissive that I enjoy spending time with, but she's not mine. The distinction is important."

"Do you have anger management issues?" Claudia asks.

"I spend most of my time with a dog and before that I spent more than twenty years with an old man who averaged about four sentences a week that weren't related to wilderness survival tactics. I'm not great at talking to new people."

"So you're just a quiet, cranky, brooding mountain man?"

"Something like that."

"I'll rephrase. You would like a session with a submissive?"

"Not just any submissive, but yes."

"Don't we have a deal? You have to tell me. The whole truth. Those are the rules."

"I've thought about dominating you."

She looks at Titus, keeps scratching his ear. She has a decent poker face when she needs one, but I know what she's thinking.

"So we're both in danger of dependency," I say.

"But you said you only need it once a year."

"With someone I have no real emotional attachment to."

"But with me it would be different."

"You aren't the only one who's been obsessing. I mentioned that."

"Then let's make one more deal. Tonight you hold me and then tomorrow, after I've gotten some sleep and a chance to stretch, you dominate me."

She's almost laughing when she says it. I know she's trying to make light of the situation. I just dropped something heavy on her plate, but that's the reason why I say, "No. No deal," immediately. "Me holding you and you submitting to me are two completely different things." I sit up and reach for my remotes.

"Why? We're both trying to work our way through some complex shit," she says as I move Titus to the floor.

"Come here before he tries to climb up again," I say.

She starts to move, then stops. "You're going to hold me."

"Yes."

"Fine, whatever." She's glaring at me again, but she slides across the couch and does the wiggling she needs to do to get comfortable against my chest. I wrap my arm around her, force myself to ignore how soft her arm is against my fingers, force myself to ignore the way her hair smells fresher than the roses she's given me. I ignore the way the simple weight of her body already makes me feel more grounded. I pull her closer and then I hand her the remotes.

"No cable, but I have every streaming app. Watch whatever you want."

"Thanks." She goes right for Netflix. "Not a complete mountain man, are you? I thought you were gonna teach me how to whittle wood into the shape of a deer while we stared at the fire and you told me about the old days before indoor plumbing." She freezes then looks up at me. "Shit. You do have indoor plumbing right?"

"Yes. And I don't know how to whittle."

"Shame."

She can't see me, but I shake my head. I settle in for what I know is going to be a long night.

✱

It's been a while, but I consider beating off in the woods while I'm out waiting for the sun to rise. I've been hard for almost ten hours. Claudia doesn't want me to hold her. She wants our bodies to meld together through our clothes. At one point I give in and slide down the length of the couch so she can lie on top of me while she watches the original *Parent Trap*.

My cock is up the entire time, wedged against her stomach. I know she feels it but she doesn't say thing. She's asleep before the movie's over. I stay up and see how these shitty parents decide to resolve this situation with their children, and then I pick her up and start to carry her to bed. Leaving her on the couch would defeat the purpose of her cross-country quest.

She wakes up when I'm halfway across the room and tells me she's fine to walk. She follows me into my bedroom. She peels off her skintight jeans and does that under the shirt maneuver to remove her bra and then she's between my sheets like she belongs there.

I watch her for a few moments before she tells me to hurry up. I go brush my teeth and change into my thermals. She's still awake when I come back, petting Titus. He's made himself comfortable on the open side of the bed. I wrestle him to the foot and slide under the covers.

Claudia moves back into my arms. I sleep better than I have in months. I spoon her the whole night, but still I'm fucking hard the whole time. She doesn't seem to mind that my cock is pressed up against her ass when I move to spoon her on my side.

In the morning I detach myself from her and head out to shoot. I take my shotgun and leave Titus behind to look over Claudia and the house. I get what I need, but the whole time I'm thinking about her. The simple grey panties she had on. The way her thighs feel against my legs. Fuck, the way she smells. I need to come up with a plan. I might have to kick her out of my house.

She's awake when I walk through the door. She's sitting on a kitchen stool having a conversation with Titus. She's wrapped herself in some patterned poncho, but she's still not wearing pants.

"Morning."

"Good morning," she says. I can't read her tone. She doesn't smile when she sees me. I realize she's looking at my gun. I put it away before I join her.

"Don't believe a word he's saying. I fed him before I left."

"I saw your note. Have you eaten yet?" she asks.

"A bit before I went out, but I usually eat again in an hour or so. I can cook or we can go down to the diner."

"Can we talk first?"

"Sure." I put my gear down on the table and join her at the island.

"I have a proposal for you and I think it might answer some questions we both have. If I'm correct, it will help us both."

"Okay. Go ahead."

"Well, one. Thank you for last night. Keeping my emotions in check, I'd like to say that spending that time with you was very helpful."

"You don't need to keep your emotions in check."

"I get that, but I feel like after last night I realized just how not okay I am. I know I showed up here unannounced, and I spent the night without even taking into consideration that you might actually have things to do today. Or that you might be in a relationship."

"I wouldn't have brought you up here if that was the case, but go on. Please."

"Still. It was nuts and rude and I'm sorry." She closes her eyes for a second and sucks in another breath. "I was serious last night. While I am not a member of a club or a *professional*, I'm not completely unfamiliar with the kind of sex you were describing." She's speaking slowly. She's considering every word.

"Part of the reason I broke up with my ex was because he stopped fucking me the way I liked him to. When I got back to New York he wasn't ready for how fucked up I was. I know he was trying to be gentle with me, but even when I was perfectly healed he turned the rough sex I preferred into this slow, measured, missionary lovemaking that I'd never signed up for. I want the rough stuff back."

My chest tightens. I fight back the frustration because she still doesn't get it, but I keep that to myself. "Okay."

"You said you needed a week, so let me give you a week. I called my best friend. She knows I'm safe and she knows where I am."

"Good."

"We take that week and we see if we can give each other what we need."

"When do you want this week to start?" I ask.

"Now."

I consider her for a moment. Her perfect, thick, golden brown thighs peeking out from under that poncho. What I could do with my fist wrapped around that long black hair. That mouth. I could fuck that mouth while I grip her long black hair. I think about her knees and what it would be like to have those big hazel eyes staring up at me while I come on her tits.

"I also understand that you are doing the honorable thing and not trying to force your desires on me, but I think you have to respect me enough as a submissive and a woman and a human being to believe me when I say this is what I want. I want to try. If this isn't something you want, I respect that too."

Fuck. She's got me there. I scrub my beard, then peel off my hat so I can scratch my head properly. She's looking at me. Waiting.

I flip the switch.

CHAPTER SEVEN

"You get dressed and pack up all your shit." Her expression drops but I'm not done yet. "We go down the mountain for breakfast and then I need to grab some condoms. We go to the Lodges and I fuck your brains out like I've been wanting to do for months now. And if you still want to submit to me, you can check out of the Lodges, follow me back up here with your rental car and we'll make a week out of it."

"And if you're just awful in bed?"

"That's where we part ways."

"As friends."

"If you want, yeah. You have my number now."

"Okay, that's fair."

"But we're going to talk about what we want to do first," I say as I walk over to the sink and turn on the faucet. I need to wash my hands. "You can always tap out, but I don't want there to be any confusion before we get started."

"Deal," she says before she launches right in. "I want you to spank me, a lot. I want you to choke me. I want you to tie me up. I want you to make me squirt if you think you can. I want to barely be able to walk whenever you're finished with me for the day."

"Anal?" I say over my shoulder as I dry my hands with a clean dish towel.

"Absolutely."

"And flogging's alright, I assume?"

That catches her off guard, but she schools her expression before she goes on. "I've never done that before, but if you're receptive to the word 'stop', then yes we can try some flogging."

I circle the island, nudge Titus out of the way, and step right into her space, right between her legs. She looks up at me with those doe eyes as I pull the sides of the poncho apart. She's still wearing that low cut t-shirt, no bra. She swallows as I pull the fabric down and expose both her tits. I don't touch them though, I just look.

"I don't have everything I want for you, but I can order some things overnight and they should be here by Monday. I'll be able to improvise until then."

Her nipples are perfect, a light brown that's blushing red as the heat crawls up her body.

"What else do you want?" she asks.

"I want you wet for me all the time. I want you nearly naked all the time."

"Why not completely naked?"

I shrug, then draw the side of my thumb over her left nipple. "I like what I like. But don't worry. There will be plenty of time for full on nudity. I want you to beg, but you don't have to worry about that too much either. I'll get you there."

"You seem so sure." She swallows again and holds back a sigh as I draw my finger over her right nipple.

"You seem pretty confident that I won't, but I'm barely touching you and I bet if I check that sweet pussy of yours, you'll be soaking wet."

"Maybe you should check."

"See, barely touched you, barely said a word and you're already asking. Begging isn't far away."

"I don't... have a response for that," she admits.

"I am on board with everything you want, but I want you to understand the difference between submission, which is what I want and sadism, which seems to be your bag."

"I know the difference. Go on."

"Alright. Well I have work do, but your job will be to properly distract me. You might not get what you want exactly when you want it, but that's part of my game. You have to show me you want it all the time."

"What else do you want?"

"I want to earn your trust. I want you to know that I will never hurt you. As rough as we get, I will always take care of you." I pinch her nipple. She yelps but the sound melts into a hiss she keeps to herself the longer I hold on. I can already see it on her face, she'll slip into place nicely. She wants this. "Are you wet for me now?"

"Yes."

I step back, releasing her nipple. "Show me."

She opens her thighs wide then slides those grey panties to the side. The fabric of the crotch is already darker with her juices. I see the bottom of a small patch of hair, but her slit is bare. She moves her fingers around, spreads her swollen lips. She starts to touch her clit.

"Did I tell you to start touching yourself?"

Her fingers still. "No."

"Lesson one. You do exactly as I tell you, not some approximation of what you think I'm getting at. Take off your underwear and go put on your jeans and your boots. Leave your bra off too."

"Okay."

"Okay is good for now, but when—if—we come back up here together, it's 'yes, Shep' or 'yes Mr. Olsen.' Understood?"

"Yes, Mr. Olsen."

"Good. Now go get ready."

She gets off the stool, a little wobbly, then walks back into the bedroom. I make sure I have my wallet and my phone and watch her as she comes back into the great room and steps into her boots.

"You ready?" I ask her as she zips up her coat.

"Yes, Shep," she says, looking me in the eye.

"Let's go." I open the front door and usher her through with a firm grip on her ass.

The diner is almost full, but Connie manages to snag us the booth I want near the back. People are looking. Claudia stands out like a sore thumb just because she's with me, but everyone is polite as usual even if they can't stop staring. With a hand on her back, I guide Claudia into the side of the booth facing the back wall.

"Sit here and keep your jacket on."

She doesn't respond, but she obeys.

Connie brings our menus and Claudia hesitates for a moment when she's asked what she would like. I tell her to go on and order what she wants.

"With your consent, I might be in control," I say when we're alone again. "But I will never tell you what to eat. That's ridiculous."

"I would have to agree with you there." She glances over her shoulder, but no one is looking at us. Everyone has turned back to their own meals and conversations.

"Show me your tits. Pull down your shirt. Don't worry. No one can see you." The booth backs are high and she's facing the rear wall of the place. This is a show for me and me only.

She hesitates for a moment, then slips her tits out of her top. She sits back to keep her nipples from touching the metal edge that wraps around the table. The tips are hard either way though.

"Do you like having your nipples fucked with?"

She swallows. "Yes. They are pretty sensitive."

"Can you come if I play with them just right?"

"I've been close."

"We'll have to test that out. Tell me more about yourself. We don't have to talk about what happened, but like you said, we should know each other."

"Keep it basic and ice breakery," she says. Her voice wavers. She's a ballsy chick, but she's not used to being exposed like this. Whether anyone can see her or not.

"Yeah, that'll work. Close your jacket," I say as I see Connie come out from behind the counter. Claudia panics even though she has plenty of time to cover up. She's concealed when our food is deposited on the table.

"Get you guys anything else?" Connie asks with a bright smile. I defer to Claudia.

"No, I'm fine thank you."

"You just holler if you change your mind." We thank her and Connie pats Claudia on the shoulder before she heads back up front.

"Tits out again," I say. "I want to look at them while I eat. You were saying." I take a bite of my pancakes and wait for her to answer.

"Um, I'm a Gemini? My dad was Swedish and my mom was from Grenada. We lived there until I was seven. I'm allergic to mango. Which is a shame because I love it."

"You allergic to anything else?" I say between bites. She hasn't touched her waffle or her eggs yet.

"No."

"Just like I'm not going to tell you what to eat, I'm not going to stop you from eating. You can eat and talk. I know you're hungry."

"Right." She picks up her fork. I decide to do the talking until most of her food is gone.

"I'm an Aquarius. I've never read my horoscope so don't expect me to know what that means." She smiles and I know she has no clue how long I'm going to spend kissing her once we leave this place.

"I'm technically an only child even though my parents have three more kids. I've never met them. Don't worry. I'm not torn up about it."

"Okay," she says, her tone skeptical around a mouthful of eggs.

"I'm six-six if you were wondering. Even though I live in the woods, I hate camping."

"Me too," she takes a sip of her water. "Can I put my boobs away?"

"No."

She scowls at me but continues eating.

"I'm really hard right now. You wouldn't want to ruin that for me, would you?"

That heat spreads across her chest again, up to her face. "No. But I don't think it's fair."

I reach into my glass and grab a piece of ice. "Scoot forward. You don't think what is fair?"

She gives me another confused look, but slides to the edge of the bench like I told her to. "I don't think it's fair that you've seen my—" she breaks off as I take the ice and rub it across her nipple. She jerks away a fraction of an inch, then holds still as I rub it around, letting it melt between our body heat.

"Go on." I grab another piece of ice and rub it around her other nipple. I know she's just soaked her pants by the way her eyes roll back in her head. "You can speak and enjoy this at the same time. Finish what you were saying."

She licks her lips, then winces as I give her wet nipple a little squeeze. "I don't think it's fair that you've seen my boobs and my pussy and I haven't seen this hard dick you speak of."

I release her nipple and lick the water off my fingers before I turn back to my breakfast.

"Do you want to see my cock?"

"Yeah. I do."

"Finish eating and we'll make that happen."

I watch her as she reaches for more of her waffle. She pauses. "We don't have to stop for condoms," she says. "I always carry them with me."

That makes me pause, but in a good way. "I always appreciate a woman who's prepared."

We finish our meal in near silence. The only sounds between us are Claudia's hisses and moans. I can't stop playing with her tits.

*

I don't know who's working at the front desk. Don't know, don't care. We head right to Claudia's cabin. I do my best not to kick open the door and wait for her to dig the key out of her purse with her shaky hands. I fingered her through her jeans on the ride over and she's about to come any second.

I slam the door behind me the minute we're inside and start taking off my clothes. She follows my lead.

"Is this a good moment for a completely naked situation?" she asks.

"Yes and those condoms would come in handy right now."

"Right." I finish stripping as she digs them up. She shoves three different types into my hands then flips on the bed and starts tearing off her boots. Her jeans come flying off just as quickly. She's laying in the center of the bed, ass naked by the time I'm sheathed up.

"You think you're just gonna lay back and enjoy this?" I say. I'm stroking myself.

She sits up. "I was waiting for orders."

"Come here."

"Yes, Shep." She stands off the bed and crosses the room to me.

"You joke now," I say, as I lightly wrap my hand around her throat. I look in her hazel eyes and my cock twitches when that hint of fear flashes across her face. She swallows. I feel her throat work against my palm.

"But?"

"You'll see. Stroke my cock." She obeys, groping for it blindly as I keep my grip on her neck until her fingers are wrapped around me. I take a deep breath, keeping my eyes trained on her as I remind my body that I'm not fifteen anymore and nutting in her hands after one touch would not be a good way to convince her she wants to spend the week with me.

"Is that enough?" I ask her.

"More than enough."

"Good," I say and then I do something I've been wanting to do, aching to do, for longer than I'd like to admit. I kiss her.

Her lips feel as good as they look. Soft and full. I drop my hand from her throat and wrap my arms around her smaller frame. I grip her perfect ass. Her hand is still moving between our bodies, stroking my dick up and down in perfect sync to the way her tongue has just invaded my mouth. She pushes closer, whimpering against my lips as I suck her in. I'm fucking done. I pull away long enough to grab one of the chairs shoved under the kitchenette table. I sit, test its weight, then reach for her.

"Sit," I say.

She straddles me, and wraps her arms around my shoulders. I have more orders, but she's kissing me again, grinding her clit against my dick.

"You want it," I say against her lips.

"Yes."

"Ask nicely."

"Please."

I lift her up and her eyes go wide as I support her full weight with one arm and press the head of my cock against her slit with my other hand.

"Please what? I want to hear you say it." I push up just a little, even though she hasn't given me what I want yet. She groans as my cock starts to spread her open.

"Please fuck me, Shep."

"Say it again."

"Please. Shep. Cut the bullshit and just fuck me already."

I laugh against her ear and then push in deep. Our twin "Fuck!"s are absorbed by the old walls of the place.

I hold her still for just a second. It's too much, how fucking tight her pussy is, and I know how big my cock is. She needs a second to adjust. I pull back and smooth her hair away from her face. Her eyes blink open.

"You okay?" I ask.

"Yes." She swallows. "Yeah, I'm fine. Your dick is huge. Huge is definitely a theme in your life."

I chuckle again. "It is. You tell me if you need me to stop."

"I will. Don't stop now. Definitely don't stop now."

I rock my hips forward and back, forward and back, deep, but nice and slow. Claudia holds still for a few moments, but she finds the rhythm I'm setting and starts to push back, taking me deep into her tight, wet cunt.

"Tell me," I say before I kiss her again. We kiss for a while, me fucking her, her fucking me in this chair that I can already tell is going to give under our weight any second. I can't make myself stand up. I don't want anything about this to change. I give us both some air, lean her back a bit and grab one of those ripe tits. I suck her nipple into my mouth, tug on it a little with my teeth.

"Oh shit. Fuck," she moans.

"Tell me," I say again as I switch to her other tit. "Tell me if you like it."

"I do, I do. Jesus, Shep. It feels so fucking good."

The chair snaps. Claudia screams. I catch us with an arm on the table. It starts tilting until I lean away from it. I'm still deep inside her cunt. I drop into a squat, to catch my balance. I hold on to her.

"Are you okay?"

"Oh my god!" She buries her face against my neck and I realize she's laughing.

"You okay?" I ask again. I stand carefully and wrap my around arm around her. She's clinging to me with all her might either way. I'd have to pry her loose.

"Yeah. I'm fine."

"Do we need to take a break?"

"No. Let's just move this to the bed."

"Okay. Hold on."

I cross the room. "Oh god, that feels so weird," she says against my beard. "I can feel like every inch of you moving. Stay inside."

"Don't let go."

I kneel on the bed and feel myself slipping out of her tight, wet grip. She holds on, long enough for me to deposit us on the covers and pick up the pace right where we left off. Her laughter quickly turns to something else. I realize I like the sound of her laugh as much as I like the sound of her moans.

She kisses me again as I pound in and out. Soon all the humor is gone and she's back to begging. She claws at my shoulders. I rear back, grab the backs of her thighs and push her knees to her chest. I need to go deep. I need her to know that I'm not fucking around. I mean business. If she decides to stay, it can be all this and more. I'll learn her body, learn what she really needs.

I shut off my mind before those thoughts go any further. She's coming.

She doesn't say my name. Just whimpers an "Oh fuck. Fuck. Fuck." as her head digs back into the pillows.

I don't let up. I pull her legs together and put them over my right shoulder. I dig deeper, pound harder. Her hands find my forearms. I feel her clenching around me, bearing down. I feel her coming again on my lap.

I don't let up.

She makes a strangled noise. She arches hard against me. There's more. Her juices soak my balls. I can't hold on any longer. I come my fucking brains out. When I come back to my senses, I gently ease out of her body and slide onto the bed beside her. She's still trembling. After I ditch the condom in the bedside trash can, I look her up and down, carefully gauging how and where I can touch her. I wrap my arm around her waist and pull her close. She rolls into me and buries her head in my chest.

We're both quiet for a long time. I'm looking at her. Her eyes are closed. We both need a second. I consider what else I need and how long I can wait to get an answer. I try to give her the time she needs.

She scoots closer. I run my fingers through her hair. I kiss her face. She turns her head and kisses my mouth.

When she pulls away she buries her nose in my chest hair. I get it. She's not in the mood for eye contact.

"I can't remember the last time I came that hard," she says.

"I try not to oversell it," I say.

"You didn't."

I squeeze my eyes shut. I can feel the drop coming. Or maybe the opposite. I can't stay in this bed much longer. I need to know. "So."

She glances up at me. "So."

"What would you like to do?"

"Don't want to give a girl much time to think, do you?"

I keep my mouth shut because I know whatever I say will make her think I have anger issues again. She reaches up and runs her fingers over my shoulder. She's looking at my tattoo. It's not small.

"One week, right?"

"Yeah."

She doesn't say anything. I'm not in the mood for a stalemate.

"I thought we had a deal. Tell me what you're thinking," I say.

"Can I get a few rainchecks worked into our deal? I'll tell you, but just not right now. Okay?" I think about what she's going through. Why she's here.

"Yeah. I think that's pretty fair."

"I want to stay," she says. "I'll come back up the mountain with you."

CHAPTER EIGHT

I mention that Titus is still up at the house alone and Claudia mentions that maybe we've overstayed our naked welcome on motel sheets. I wait for her to use the bathroom and grab all her shit, and we go. Some guy I've never met named Jake is working the desk at the Lodges and maybe he checked Claudia in or some shit, but he's eyeing me like something's up. I don't owe him an explanation for why she's leaving with me.

I double check to make sure she has all of her things loaded in the trunk of her rental car and then I tell her to follow me to the market because once we get up to my place we're not coming back down until what I plan to order for Claudia arrives at the post office. By the time we check out, I give up all illusions that anyone will even notice that Claudia is with me. Not that it crosses my mind to keep her some kind of secret, but the mountain gets plenty of visitors. She's no different.

We run into Rich in the bread aisle and he's not subtle in the way he greets Claudia or the way he waggles his eyebrows at me. If he wasn't practically my cousin I would punch him in the face. I know the longer she stays in town the more people are going to talk, but I can't bring myself to give much of a shit, especially when I look at her.

It takes twice as long as usual to get back to my place. I go slow so she can follow easily. When I get to my road, I see the gate is open. I know I closed it, but I have an idea who's looking for me. May-Bell's red SUV is on my lawn when we pull into the clearing of my property.

"I'd tease you for driving like an old man," Claudia says when she climbs out of her rental. "But that road is no joke."

"Safety first. Leave your stuff. I'll come out and get it in a minute."

"I got it," she says as she walks around to the trunk. She nods up toward the house. "You have a visitor."

I don't turn around. "Come on," I say once she's loaded down with all her bags.

We walk up to the front door and sure enough May-Bell is waiting on my porch. She's got a few dishes in her hands. She doesn't look amused with me, but she has a smile for Claudia.

"Shep," she says.

I lean down and kiss her cheek. "Hi May. This is Claudia."

"For conversation's sake, I'm this one's aunt. It's nice to meet you. How are you doing?" May-Bell says as I open the front door.

"I'm well, thank you."

"Come on in." I nudge Titus out of the way. He's always glad to see me, but he's been hyper as a bag of dicks since Claudia showed up. It's hard to ignore.

"Just brought you a little something to eat. There's plenty for two," May says.

"Thank you," I say as I put the groceries down on the counter. Claudia slides her things over in the corner by the fireplace.

"So how long are you in town?" May asks Claudia.

"Uh, about a week. I was out here about six months ago, but my trip was cut short. I just—"

"You don't—you don't have to do all that. I know who you are."

Claudia's back snaps straight and her eyes flash between me and May. "Oh. Well. I wanted to see Shep again. I didn't really get a chance to talk to him before I went home. And we forgot to exchange numbers," she adds quickly.

"Well it's nice to have you back in one piece. I can't imagine what you went through. My husband, Jad and I live down the road a ways. Make sure Shep here gives you my number. It works out here with the wireless fi. You just call me if you need anything."

"Thank you." I can hear the confusion in her voice.

"Well I'll leave you two to the rest of your day. Shep, you want to walk me out to my car?"

"Sure thing." I grab my keys off the table and follow May-Bell to the door. I stop and kiss Claudia on the forehead. "I'll be right back."

"'Kay."

I leave the door open for Titus to follow me, but he seems way too interested in Claudia. I follow May-Bell across the lawn. She's parked right near the tree line. When she reaches the driver's door she turns on me.

"This is the girl you saved." May-Bell and Jad never laid eyes on Claudia, but they know enough. "Do I need to ask what's going on?"

"You can."

"Well?"

"What's bothering you about this?"

"I heard that she came into town to say thank you to some folks, you included. Which is lovely. It's a very sweet gesture, but—"

"She's clearly staying with me."

"Connie messaged me this morning. She said you two came down for breakfast together."

I shake my head and try not to laugh. "I should have never taught either of you how to text."

"Well it's too late. You can't take it back. You sleeping with this girl?"

"May."

"No. I'm asking. You haven't brought anyone up here since—"

"Since, I know. She came to town to see me. She's here for a few days and as much as I'd love to hang out at the Lodges, it just made more sense to come up here."

"Mhmm. Get all the privacy."

"I'm a grown man, Mrs. Tierney."

"No you're not. You're just tall."

"I should get back. Thank you for the food. I'll bring the platters back."

"Don't worry. I'll come by in a few days."

"Is there a nice way to ask you to call first?"

"I suppose that's a fair request." She tilts her cheek up for a kiss and then hops in her SUV. I wait until she's backed down the drive until I wave and head back inside. I find Claudia in the kitchen, putting away the groceries. She's on the phone. She turns and looks at me.

"He just came back—yes, mom. Hold on—no, I know," she laughs. "And I love you for it. Hold on." She drops her hand down by her side. "It's my best friend, Liz. She wants to talk to you."

I hold my palm out for her cell. "Voice verification required."

"Something like that."

"Hello?"

"Is this Shepard Olsen?"

"It is."

"Hi, yeah. Great to chat with you finally. Here's the deal. My amazing, beautiful, well-meaning friend who is the most important thing in the world to me besides my own sister, didn't tell me where the fuck she was going when she dipped out of town."

I look right at Claudia. "Did she tell you she was leaving town at all?"

"Yes, but not to track you down."

"Oh? Where did she tell you she was going?" Claudia makes a face that lets me know she knows she's been caught.

"To San Jose. To see her brother's girlfriend. Or his ex."

"I see."

"Here's what I'm gonna need from you, Mr. Olsen."

"Sure."

"Your phone number. Your home address—she's at your house right now, right?"

"Yes."

"Great. So yeah, your home address. A copy of your driver's license. I will accept a picture via text. I would also like a picture of you and Claudia together so I can see that she is in one piece."

"We can arrange all that."

"Good. If I actually trusted the police I'd send them there to do a wellness check, but she sounds normal so I figure that would be way more trouble than it's worth. Plus I don't want to get one of you shot by accident."

"I appreciate that."

"That's it. Be good to her. Or I swear to god—"

"I understand. I promise you she's in good hands. Do you want the picture of us together right now, before I give her the phone back?"

"Actually yes."

"Hold on." I grab Titus by the collar, then wave Claudia over to the couch.

"What are we doing?"

"Quick family photo so your friend knows I'm a real person and you're not dead." I sit and pull her into my lap. Titus jumps on the couch beside me. I stretch my arm out and snap two pictures. Claudia is scowling in both. "You look like you're having a real blast."

"Oh sorry." We try again and I manage not to laugh when she flashes a wide grin and a thumbs up. It takes a few seconds but I text the photo to her friend that she has saved as Mrs. Darcy.

"Photo sent."

"Got it. Thank you." She pauses. "Yeah, okay. You're kinda hot. Has that dog had its shots?"

"Yes. One hundred percent healthy and mountain rabies free. And he doesn't bite."

"Good to know. Well… Thank you. I still need all your information though."

"I'll text it over as soon as you and Claudia wrap up your conversation."

"Thank you—"

"You can call me Shep."

"Thank you, Shep. Seriously don't hurt her. I will find you and I will fuck you up."

I do laugh this time, but only because she's caught me off guard. "I promise I will return her safely to the East coast."

"Great. Let me talk to her."

"Here." I hand Claudia back her phone and start to put away the rest of her groceries. I catch a glimpse of her as she slips into the bedroom and closes the door, but not before making the "just one minute" gesture with her finger.

She's in there for longer than a minute. I put away all the groceries and set the steak for dinner in its marinade. I'm about to get back to work at my dining room table when she finally comes out of my bedroom. Titus is knocked out, but he lifts his head the minute she opens the door.

"Sorry about that."

"I'm not going to say it's okay," I tell her.

"You're right, it's not. I just didn't know how to tell her. 'I'm going to track down this guy who saved my life to see if he'll give me a hug' doesn't usually come out the way it's intended." It's funny, but I can't let this go.

"She sounds like she really cares about you."

"She does."

"We're going to send her some apology flowers today."

Her eyebrows go up.

"I'm serious. I think you really scared her and that's not cool. I might live up here all alone, but even I know when I'm in a fucked up place I have to remember that there are people who care about me."

She glares at me for a second. She's not in the mood for a lecture, but I don't give a shit. "And the last thing I need is the Feds coming back around looking for you 'cause your friend has legitimate reason to think you went missing."

That softens her expression, but her body is still tense. "You're right."

"Come here." I push back from the table and make room for her between my legs. I pull her close. I wrap my arms around her. I look up into her beautiful hazel eyes. "I understand how you feel, but you come first. Never put yourself in even questionable danger. Not for anyone."

Her gaze roams all over my face, but she won't look me in the eye. I notice the way her throat is moving. She's holding back tears. "Yeah I kinda fucked this up. I'll send her something nice and make sure I thoroughly apologize the second I get home. Is everything cool with your neighbor-aunt?"

"Yeah. She's just… concerned. Nothing to worry about though." I reach up and run my thumb over her cheek and cup her face. She leans into my hand.

"She was interesting. I thought New Yorkers had a bad rep for being ultra direct."

"It's not you at all. She's pissed at me."

"Are you sure?"

"Yes. She and Jad have looked out for me since I was a kid and she's had a hawk's eye on me since my grandfather died. She's also a really nosy old lady who knows you can set your watch by my comings and goings. Hearing that I have a visitor and didn't tell her about it is making her a little uneasy."

"Oh. Anyone else in town I should be worried about, thinking I'm disrupting your perfect mountain routine?"

"I don't think so." I know I fucked up the moment I hesitate. Dropping my hands down to her ass doesn't seem like enough to distract her from the question.

"I don't believe you, but I'll have to take your word for it. So what do we do now? I'm yours but clearly you have stuff to do," she nods toward my laptop.

"How are you feeling? Are you tired?" I give her ass another squeeze. She moves even closer and leans her stomach against my chest. It's only been hours, but I can feel how comfortable she already is with me.

She finally looks me in the eye. "I'm exhausted. Did the riverboat-sized bags under my eyes give me away?"

"No, I was thinking about the cross-country travel and sleeping in different bed part, but now that you mention it, you do look pretty terrible."

"Oh you've got jokes, do you?"

I smile at her a little. "Why don't you lay down for a while and then I'll wake you when I'm finished uploading this stuff."

She looks at the images on my computer screen. "Yeah, okay. That's a good idea."

"What's wrong?"

"Honesty is a lot harder than most people think."

"And lying or not telling me something for an unknown reason doesn't work well either."

"I'm...thinking about the time we have together."

"Yeah."

"It is limited." She pauses and I think she might bite clear through that sexy bottom lip of hers. I stand and smooth her hair back away from her face. I kiss her.

"Tell me."

"I can't, seriously. I'm not trying to keep anything back or anything, it's just... this kind of frankness is weird for me. Isn't it weird for you?"

"No."

"Well I still need some time. Maybe like forty-eight full hours to feel a little more comfortable just blurting out everything that crosses my mind."

"That's fair."

Her phone chimes and vibrates. She looks down at the screen. "It's Liz. She's waiting on your license picture. Also I can't believe you're so secluded out here, you don't have to lock your wifi."

"One less thing to remember," I say as I pull out my wallet. I throw my ID down on the table and let Claudia snap a picture.

"That's the correct address right? She's gonna look it up on Google Maps."

"Right address. Was living right here when I got my learner's permit. The address never changed."

She tries to hide a little smile, but I still catch it. I decide to let her have this one. Once she sends the picture, there's some more texting before she turns her full attention back to me.

"I should probably look into that nap. The couch okay?" she asks.

"Mind if I join you?"

"Not at all."

She goes to sit down and I gather up my computer and my drives and all the rest of the shit I need to work and set it all up on the coffee table. I grab the other blanket

May-Bell made sure I had around for guests and drape it over her lap.

She curls up beside me as I finish uploading the shots I took that morning. Before I even open my design email, she's out cold.

She sleeps the rest of the morning and the whole afternoon. I finish almost all my work, make lunch and have a conference call before she cracks an eyelid. I'm just about to get started on dinner when she wakes up. I turn from the fridge and watch her as she stretches and looks around. She looks at me and blinks a few times as she tries to get her bearings.

I almost laugh. She's looking right at me, but she looks comically confused. "You okay?"

Her eye twitches in the oddest way and I do laugh. She rubs her face then forces her eyes to open wider. "I had a dream I was in a pumpkin patch maze and it was fucking terrible. I couldn't get out and every time I thought I found the exit it would disappear."

"Aren't pumpkins pretty low to the ground?"

"Yes! And I couldn't step over them. I kept trying and my legs would only go so high." She groans and rubs her face.

"Should we break that down any further?" I say. I'm just fucking with her though.

"Oh, I know it means my brain is all fucked up right now, but I'm not paying you hourly for couch space. Can I use your shower?"

"Of course. Come on."

She follows me to the bathroom and I show her where the towels and the wash rags are. "I'll be out in the kitchen."

"I know you didn't build this shower for two, but god it's big."

"The water was hitting my chest before. I had to make some adjustments. Do you want me to join you?"

She looks me up and down for a moment. "Is it about what I want now? Sir?"

I feel myself getting hard and irritated. "This is all about what you want. You'll see that."

"Hmmm." She starts peeling off her clothes. I've already seen her naked, but I appreciate her body just as much the second time around. I need to be inside of her again, but not like this.

"Do I have to beg again?" she says. "Do I say please?" She smiles at me as piles her hair up on her head in one of those sexy as fuck ponytails and turns the shower nozzle. I glance down at her hard nipples when she turns to wet her back. My cock almost tears a hole in my jeans. I want her, but not like this.

"Get washed up and we'll figure out what we want to do tonight." I turn and walk out of the bathroom. I close the door, but I can still hear her call my name.

I'm already fucking up. I can feel it. I need air. I need to step outside. I go out the back door. Titus follows. The sun is down and the temperature has dropped. It's going to start raining again any minute. I think about going back in for my phone. I think about calling Mistress Evelyn, but I know what she'll say. She'll tell me to take a deep breath. She'll tell me there's nothing wrong with taking a step back. She'll tell me that Claudia or any submissive deserves my best when they are in my care. She'll tell me to tell the truth.

I try not to think about Sarah, but it's impossible. She's in every fucking corner of my mind and every fucking wall of this house. When Titus and I step back inside, I can hear the shower is off. I find Claudia in my bedroom. She's still naked, digging through one of her bags. The towel she'd borrowed is wrapped around her hair. I look at her body, her brown skin tinted red from the heat of the water.

"Hey," I say.

She turns and looks at me. "Did I say something wrong?"

I look at the bottle of lotion in her hand. "No. And I need to apologize for making you feel like you did. I need to be honest with you right now because I don't think I can change my whole personality overnight. Just like you can't be boldly honest, I can't predict when this … shitty part of my past is going to spring up in my mind and turn me into a massive dick."

She smirks a bit. "Okay. Go on."

"Come with me a sec."

"Are we going outside? Do I need to put on boots at least?"

"No. You're fine just the way you are." I hold out my hand. She crosses the room and wraps her fingers around mine. I lead her into my office that I never use.

I give her a minute to look around at the boxes I have stacked in the corner, the loft bed that's stacked with odds and ends that belonged to my grandparents. Some of my mom's things. The dust on most of the surfaces is pretty obvious to me. I'm not sure if she sees it.

"This was my room," I tell her. "It was my mom's room and when I remodeled the house it was going to be a nursery."

Her head snaps in my direction and I realize what I just said.

"I didn't lose a kid."

"Oh. Okay. What happened?"

"I had a girlfriend who I wanted to marry. She knew how things were for me. What I... need."

"She couldn't do it?"

"No, she couldn't but she made me think she could and she made me think she wanted to. I tried to turn this place into a real home for us. I proposed, but she split with some guy who she met online."

"Yeah, that's shitty."

"I'm not trying to get you to take her place. You're only staying a week."

"Oh. I didn't think that."

"Nah, I just—I know how to dominate someone who is already in that headspace. The, uh, the woman I deal with in LA is a submissive twenty-four seven. She's been in the lifestyle for over ten years. I have it very easy with her. I know I take that for granted. I don't know how to dominate someone who could possibly just be going along with what I want just to make me happy. Or for whatever reason. I know it feels like we're going in circles here, but when you said 'Sir,' that's why it reminded me of her. Of my ex. She used to tease me like that. When we finally talked about shit, she said it was my fault. I was pushing her."

"You don't think I want you to dominate me for real."

"It's just where my head's at."

She steps in front of me and puts her hand on my chest. "If you did believe that I wanted you to dominate me, what would you do to me right now?"

I figure I might as well tell the truth. There's no harm in hypotheticals. "I'd have you get on your knees right now and I'd fuck your mouth."

"Okay."

I watch Claudia as she pulls the towel off her hair and starts to fold it in half. She folds it in half again. She steps back just enough to place it on the floor. Then she kneels in front of me.

"You were saying?"

CHAPTER NINE

CLAUDIA

Shep seems a whole lot taller when I'm down on my knees. A lot more imposing than the gentle giant he's proved himself to be in the last twenty-four hours. His brain also seems to be working overtime because he's just staring at me. Whatever happened between him and his ex really did a number on him, but I get it, finally. He takes this submission thing very seriously and it only works for him when he's with people who take it seriously too. I like to tease him. I like to tease everyone, it's my nature, but I'm not trying to make fun of him.

I know he means business when he says this is the only way he can do things. I don't want to freak Shep out by letting him know that I have no fucking idea what I'm doing. I don't want to scare him off. I want him to fuck me. I want him to show me what he needs, especially since he's already giving me exactly what I need. Focus. Attention. A touch that isn't hesitant and incomplete. We made a deal. He wants me on my knees. He's got me. On my knees.

He's still looking down at me. I see his eyes roam all over my body. My pussy is totally into it, swelling and soaking already and he hasn't even touched me. My hair's still wet. I can feel water dripping down my back, down the crack of my ass. He's still looking. He's so concerned about what I actually want. I want him to touch me. Getting my mouth fucked doesn't sound half bad either. But I'm seeing now, I need to play his game a certain way.

He's still looking at me. I can see his cock growing in his jeans, inches away from my face, but he hasn't said a word.

"I'm on my knees," I say. "What happens next?"

He licks his lips. "You'd take my cock out of my pants."

I reach up and undo his belt, then pull down his zipper. His erection slips into my hand as I reach into the slit in his boxer briefs. I didn't get to touch him before, down at the motel. Not the way I wanted to, but I can do what I want now. I start to stroke him. Shep swallows and licks his lips again.

"Put your hands on my thighs and leave them there." I do what he says. "Just like that."

Shep takes his dick in his hand and starts to stroke himself. "Open your mouth." I do what he says. "Good. Just like that." I watch his face as he slips it between my lips. There's no way I can take him all the way in. He's just thick enough that I know my jaw will be pleasantly sore when he's done, but he's too long. There's too much of him. He knows. He gently nudges the back of my throat. I close my lips around him, move my tongue. My pussy clenches. It's been too long.

"You open to tips?" I almost choke on him when I try not to laugh, but I manage to nod. "Bad choice of words. Simple suggestion. Breathe, but don't try to swallow. It'll make this a lot easier." Of course my body instantly tries to swallow, but he must have guessed I would because he pulls back just enough that I don't choke on the head of his massive erection.

He pushes forward again, still gripping the base of his cock. I help him this time, bobbing and tilting my head a little to take more of him. When I pull back, I make sure I use my tongue, swirl it around every hot veiny inch I can reach. I suck on the head, lick the saltiness from the slit. He groans. He moves forward again. I match his rhythm, glancing up before I focus back on his thick patch of dark hair at the base of his shaft.

He starts to move a little faster, but it's not anything I can't handle. I haven't told him how much I like sucking cock and how many fights Jason and I had over simple things like blow jobs because he thought I wasn't ready for regular sex yet. Shep has no idea how much I've missed this. He leans over me and gathers up my hair. His cock slips out of my mouth as he's reaching. I take a moment to catch my breath.

"You okay?" he asks me.

I nod and say "Mhmm." He runs his thumb over my bottom lip. I flick my tongue out and lick over the callused skin there. He's looking down at me, his gaze turning into somewhat of a glare. I have a feeling I'm about to be in a world of hurt.

I pull back as much as I can. He's still gripping my hair. "Would I have a safe word or something? If we were doing this the way you wanted to."

He stares at me some more. He's back with his thumb, pushing in and out of my mouth, rubbing it all over my bottom lip. I bite down a little before I go back to sucking it. I have no idea why this turns me on, but it does. My pussy is fucking aching. I want to touch myself.

"No," he finally says. "I would just keep fucking you and fucking you. And you would like it. You wouldn't need to tap out, but I'm not that crazy."

He bends over and I'm forced to drop my hands from his thighs. He pulls my head back, hard. I wince, but it's more shock than pain and then his mouth is on mine. I fucking love the way he kisses. I should tell him at some point, I think and then I can't think. All thought leaves my head. It's just a sea of moaning sounds and desperately pleading. I'm not sure whether I'm saying anything out loud.

He pulls away. I almost ask him to come back. I want more. Instead I lick my lips, lick up the taste of his mouth on mine and look up into his dark brown eyes.

"Put your hands back where they were. If you want me to stop just pinch my thigh. Okay?"

I nod and find my voice. "Okay."

He nods and then he's gripping his cock again and this time he isn't gentle. He shoves it back in my mouth. I gag a bit in the split second before he pulls back and then he's pushing back in again. He's fucking my mouth hard and fast, pumping in and out. I'm trying to keep up with him but I can't. I don't know why, but I start to panic.

I want him to fuck my mouth. I want to suck his cock until he's coming down my throat, but when his grip on my hair starts to hurt, when it becomes clear that he's holding me perfectly still so I won't work against the thrusting of his hips, I find myself scratching for purchase on his jeans. I'm not pinching him, but I'm pushing back. There's just too much of him. I need room to breathe if this is going to work.

"Look at me," he says. I realize then that my eyes have been darting all over the place. I've been looking everywhere but at Shep's face. He focuses on my eyes. "Just look at me. There you go. Don't look anywhere else. You're fine. Right?" He's still pumping in and out of my mouth, but I realize what he's saying is true. He's not hurting me at all. I'm just freaking out because this is all new to me. "Breathe, but don't swallow. That's a girl. Just like that."

I glance down at his pelvis again and his fingers are instantly on my chin, even though he still has a firm grip on my hair. "Uh-uh. Eyes up here. Yeah. Look at me. Do you want me to stop?" he asks.

I shake my head the best I can.

"Good. Just keep sucking." Something about the way his voice sounds when he says those words has my pussy clenching again. I do my best to relax. I hold on to his thigh as he pumps in and out of my mouth. I'm doing what he says, watching the expressions on his face as he works so hard to stay in control. He's trying not to come.

Before I realize it, drool is running down my chin and between my breasts. Another thing that shouldn't be turning me on so much, but it does. I moan. Shep seems to like that. He makes his own sound, maybe something close to "Fuck." He fucks my mouth a little harder. I start to gag on it, over and over, but I don't want him to stop. I just worry about breathing and licking along the length of him.

"Suck it," he finally says. And I do, even though he still has my hair wrapped in his fist. I bob my head back and forth, taking as much of him as I can. "Fuck," he groans in that very specific way. I know he's close to coming. I'm about to go for my finishing move, the signature lick and suck technique that I know will have him coming down the back of my throat, but he stops me before I can and he's fucking my face again.

I make a noise. A high-pitched moan and maybe that's what does the trick. He holds still and grips the base of his dick. He starts coming in my mouth. I close my lips around him and start sucking again even though he hasn't told me to. He groans even louder and bends over me and shoot more into my mouth. Now I do swallow. I can't help myself. I suck and swallow and suck and swallow until he pulls away from me with a gasp and sinks against the dust-covered desk along the far wall.

I stare at him as he rubs his beard and utters a few swears. I sit back and my hand automatically goes between my legs. I don't realize how hard I'm rubbing my clit until another breathy moan slips out of me.

"You want to come?" he asks.

I nod. "Yeah."

Shep stuffs himself back in his pants and zips up his fly. He's up in a flash and he has me by the hair again. "Get up," he says firmly. I push off the floor, but really he's picking me up. The back of my head fills with a pleasurable ache, but I can't call it pain. It feels like every point on my body is wired directly to my cunt. I stumble forward a few steps as he turns me toward the door, but let him march me to the bedroom with ease. He sits down on the bed and propels me over his lap. I don't have time to think before his hand comes down on my ass.

"Jesus!" I scream, and he's smacking my ass again. I wiggle and try to cover my butt with my hands but he lets go of my hair and grabs both of my wrists in one of his hands.

"Stop moving," he says, his tone deathly serious. His fingers slide between my legs and he's pushing his way into my pussy. I cry out and push down on his hand. I don't know whether or not he's fucking me or if I'm fucking myself using him, but I can feel myself desperately grinding my hips.

When he pulls his hand away, I think I might die, but he flips me over and before I can open my eyes, he's on the floor and his head is between my legs. His mouth is on my clit. It's my turn to dig my fingers into his hair. I realize he's still wearing his beanie. I pull it off and toss it somewhere. My fingers slide into his thick curls that he should never hide under a hat and pull him closer. It's my turn.

There was something between us earlier, something about not overselling it. Shep's mouth is lethal. A gift. He knows exactly how to eat me, how to use his fingers inside me. There's no way I can just lay back and enjoy this. I'm coming in minutes, practically humping his face as he holds me down with a firm hand on my hip. I call out his name. I pull him closer until I can't take any more.

I flop back on the sheets. I try to breathe. I look up when Shep rises to his feet. He swipes his beard in the crudest way, then reaches for his hat from the foot of the bed. He slides it on his head all casual like. He doesn't look at me.

"Finish cleaning up," he says. And then he turns and leaves.

✱

When I catch my breath, I head back into the bathroom and rinse all the drool off my chest and rinse out my mouth. Assuming we're going to be in for the rest of the night, I settle on a sweater and some leggings before I head back into the massive living/dining area that makes up most of the house. Shep is at the kitchen counter cutting up two massive steaks. There's already a freshly tossed salad and some mashed potatoes and gravy ready to go.

"You cooked all this?" I ask.

"Yeah. Like I said, it's a pain in the ass to drive down the mountain just to eat. Had to perfect my favorites."

I climb up on the stool. "So I see what you were saying."

"About?" He glances up from his knife work.

"About the difference between saying you want to submit and actually doing it."

He puts down the cutlery and braces himself on the edge of the island. He looks me right in the eye. "Do you regret it?"

"No. I liked it. A lot. I just didn't realize how in control I was before. I... I usually initiated everything with my ex and with guys before him."

"Do you want to stop?"

I bite my lip and shake my head. "I liked the way we did things today. It was just shocking. Yeah, shocking is the right word. I'm gonna cliché you all the way up and say that I've never been with a guy like you before. Like ever."

"I've never been with anyone like you either."

"First of firsts, huh?"

"I'm still not doing this the way I want to," he says, like he's still so conflicted.

"What do you mean?"

"There's this thing called aftercare. When you finish a scene like we just did I'm supposed to check in with you, make sure you're good. Stay with you when you're coming down from the endorphins—"

"I'm fine," I say. "I mean you didn't have to leave the room, but I was fine. I'm fine now."

"There are actually rules to this, so no it's not fine for me to leave you alone like that. If my—" he stops himself, then rocks back a step and looks at the floor. "There are rules." He comes around the counter and gently slides his hand around the side of my neck and up under my hair, which is still damp. Goosebumps break out all over me at his touch. "Did I hurt you?"

"No."

"Are you sore anywhere?" He starts to massage the base of my scalp. My eyes roll closed and I sigh. He asks me again. "Claudia. Listen to me. Just tell me. Are you sore?"

"My knees a little and my mouth, but not in a bad way." I lean into his touch. "When I say I'm fine, I mean it. Are *you* okay?"

"Feeling different levels of guilt, but I'm fine."

I reach up and wrap my hand around his wrist. "Listen to me. You have nothing to feel guilty about. I liked what we did. I want to do it again. I want to do more."

"You're sure?"

"Yes."

"Alright."

"I'm sorry things went down that way with your ex. I know how difficult things can be with exes, but as we get to know each other better one thing you have to know about me, even if I have a hard time telling you my deepest darkest secrets, I am horrible at doing things that I don't want to do. I wanted you to show me how to submit to you. I want you to show me more. I liked what we did, a lot."

This time I lean up and kiss him. I knew I was in trouble the moment I booked my flight, but now I'm in real danger. We've made a deal and yeah there are rules, but there's some stuff I just can't tell him. Like how the way he kisses makes me lose all my fucking sense. Or how he has the best mouth and the best dick I've ever experienced in my whole life. I know I mean for this to be a short, reassuring kiss, but I find myself wrapping my arms around his waist and pulling him close. He gathers up my hair again, but this time he's extra gentle.

When I break our kiss I can't help but laugh at the look on his face. His brow is all scrunched up. He's looking at my lips and licking his own. "You don't like artificial pineapple flavor?"

"Is that what that is?"

"Yeah, it's my favorite after shower lip balm."

He rubs his finger along his lip like it's gonna come away a different color or something.

I sigh and slip my hand under the hem of his shirt. "What am I going to do with you?"

"Tonight. We're shopping."

"For what?"

"Bondage rope. A few different gags. A flogger. You have any sexy lingerie in your luggage?"

I laugh a little because it wouldn't be all that far fetched if I said I thought about packing some. "No. Just regular draws."

"We'll have to get you some."

"I see. And what else?"

"Some toys."

"Toys?" I say, kind of feigning shock. What the hell does this boy have in mind?

"As much as I would love to be able to fuck you all day long, my dick needs time to recover. With the right toys though..."

"Uh huh. Go on."

"With the right toys, I'll be able to keep you wet and ready all day long." My cunt swells at the thought.

"Are you going to be good to go again tonight?" I ask.

"Are you asking me if I'll be able to fuck you again?"

"Yes."

"Is that what you want?"

"Yes."

"Then we'll have to work something out. Are you hungry?"

"I'm starved. Are you going to let me keep my tits in my shirt during this meal?"

"Are you going to pretend you didn't like that?" He steps back around the counter and starts portioning out the steak and potatoes until I'm satisfied with what's piled on my plate.

"I mean, I didn't *hate* it."

I serve myself some salad, then watch him as he prepares his own plate. I watch him some more as he comes around the counter with the two beers he's just pulled out of the fridge and sits down beside me at the island. "Mhmm. That's what I thought. I hope you enjoy my epic cooking skills."

I take a bite of the steak which is smothered in this mouthwatering garlic butter. I glare at him. He watches me as I chew. When I swallow I debate punching him in the arm.

"Well?"

"Could you cook like this when your ex was in the picture?"

"I started cooking like this when I was twelve, so yeah."

I keep from saying what's on the tip of my tongue and take another bite. He nudges my leg under the counter.

To each their own, but I cannot for the life of me imagine what the fuck his ex was thinking when she left this perfect man.

CHAPTER TEN

SHEP

"I want to tell my friends about this steak, but I'm afraid at least four or five of them would show up at your door," she says. She's almost cleaned her plate twice. I'm thinking about asking her if she wants thirds, but she's slowing down. She talked through most of the meal, giving me plenty of time to eat my own dinner.

"If they can find it. You save any room for dessert?" I ask, looking at her nearly clear plate.

"There's dessert?"

"May-Bell is a baking machine."

"I'm stuffed. It's so much easier to eat when someone isn't playing with your tits—What are you thinking?" she asks with a smile. "You may be quiet and brooding, but your expressions give you up every time."

"I was just thinking that I should make you spend the rest of our meals completely naked."

"You're a pervert," she says. Her glare is full of mocking.

"I'm pretty sure you'd enjoy it though. It can be something we work on together. You being naked for me isn't something to be ashamed of."

"But just for you? Not anyone else." I don't tell her how my body reacts to the thought.

"Yeah."

"Mhmm." She pushes her plate away. "There's this place in Brooklyn that serves up the best cut of meat I've ever had, but you might have them beat."

"High praise. I'm glad you enjoyed it."

"Have you been to New York?"

I laugh. "You're asking if I've ever been off the mountain."

"I mean, I know you have. You have your sexcapades in LA, but—"

"I went to RISD and we went to the city pretty frequently."

"Oh."

"I'm not some backwoods yokel. Though I have few friends who are and they are pretty solid people," I say.

"You know I didn't mean that. I just meant you seem so comfortable here and you mentioned how much of a pain it is to go up and down and up and down. What made you settle back up here after getting a taste of city life?" she asks.

"I had a great experience on the east coast, but —"

"Hmm, you can take the man out of the mountains, but you can't—"

"Pretty much. And I was homesick. I missed my grandfather a lot."

"You were really close with him, weren't you?"

"I mean you see how big this place is. Almost twenty years up here just the two of us…and he was a good father. I'm pretty sure my mom felt good about leaving me with him. He taught me everything I know and gave me the tools to figure out the rest."

I look up as Titus starts sniffing around the front door. I owe him for the distraction. I don't like thinking about my grandfather too much these days. "I have to let him out. You okay here for a bit?"

"Yeah, sure. I'll clean up."

"You don't have to," I say as I stand. "You're my guest. I'll handle it when I get back." I fight the urge to kiss her and grab my jacket off the back of the couch. "Back in a minute."

She flashes me a half smile before I close the front door behind me. It's getting toward full night outside. The weather has been unpredictable, but the sun is setting earlier and earlier. The security lights flash on the moment I step off the porch and Titus takes off for his favorite copse of trees at the bottom of the driveway.

Titus handles his business and then after a few minutes it's clear he's just making up for the fact that I've been ignoring him all day. He comes when I call him and tries to race me back to the front door. I owe him a long walk over the weekend.

When I open the door, I find Claudia frantically searching through my cabinets and drawers. She's cleared the island and washed most of our dinner dishes.

"What are you looking for?"

"Dish towels. I don't know how you live up here alone."

"Other side of the sink. Top drawer. What do you mean?" She ignores me at first and digs out a towel and starts drying. I walk over to the sink and fill Titus's bowl. I keep my eyes on Claudia as I move back toward the island to get the rest of the potatoes. She starts drying our plates and our silverware and I decide to wait. She figures out where everything goes and finally she stops moving.

She won't look at me though. I wait longer. She turns around and takes a deep breath.

"You were gone like five minutes and I couldn't handle it." The words spill out and her tone is all fucked up, like she's telling me a funny anecdote and not coming down from a panic attack. "I tried to wash all the dishes, but I couldn't hear anything over the sound of the water. Freaked me out a little."

"Are you okay?"

"Yeah. It's just—the city's so loud. It's so quiet up here. But I'm glad you're back. Jesus, I'm fucked up."

"No, you're not," I say.

"Yeah, you say that but you don't know what's going through my head."

"I opened the floor for communication."

She almost rolls her eyes, but it turns into more of a wince. "Fine. I'm scared. There."

"What are you scared about?"

"Well first I had this really sickening thought of you walking out into the woods and not coming back. And then when I heard you call Titus, I started thinking about just how scared I am—you know, in general."

"I'm back. I came back."

"I know you did. Still having some issues though."

I don't know what to do. I keep asking her, pushing her, but maybe the talking isn't actually helping. I don't need more reminders that maybe we're making a mistake here.

"This," she blurts out. "The dependency thing. I don't trust the way I feel right now at all."

"How—"

"You make me feel so good, Shep!" she shouts at me. It's enough to shut me up. I pull out the stool and sit. "This is just—this must seriously be what crackheads feel like. Honestly. There's that voice in my head—ugh!" I watch her as she presses the heels of her hands against her eyes and then spins toward the sink. Her face is a little splotchy when she turns back around.

"I need to get help. I need to get on with my life, but just being around you makes me feel so much better. I don't know why," she says sounding a little disgusted and then she smiles. "I mean you're not all that great."

"I'll try to suck a little more."

"Could you?!" She sighs and leans back against the counter and wraps her arms around her waist. "What I want doesn't make sense. It's like there's this treadmill and there's this monster chasing me and instead of facing the monster or even assessing it for weak spots, I want you to hop on the treadmill with me."

I can feel my jaw clench. "We're already on that treadmill together."

"No, we're not."

"I think we are."

"I'm fucking falling for you, Shep and it makes no sense. You want to know why?"

"Sure. Shoot."

"You're made up. Tall, scruffy, brooding, you know when to admit you're wrong, I think. Surely there's something I have to hate about you," she says. "Do you know how bad that is? Do you have any idea how afraid I am that it's going to get worse? I cannot trust myself right now. You're exceeding my wildest coping mechanism fantasies and I know it's too good to be true. And even if it isn't, the clock is ticking—"

"Do you want to leave?" It's the only thing I can think to say. "I feel like every minute you're here I'm fucking something up or causing you pain."

"You're not. I'm sorry. And no. I can't. I need this week as badly as you do. I want you to fuck me again. I want to…"

"You want me to what?"

"Nothing," she says as she shakes her head. She won't look at me.

"Claudia. You want me to what?" She still doesn't answer. I cross the room and step right into her personal space. I park my hands on the counter on either side of her perfect body. She sags closer and I can feel the heat coming off her.

"Tell me."

She shakes her head again. "I know it's not wrong, but it's coming from the worst place. Maybe it is wrong. I don't know."

I take a risk and go for her throat again. I slip my hand up around the front of her neck, tilt her chin up. My cock goes hard when I hear her little gasp. She looks up at me, her big hazel eyes rimmed red with tears ready to spill over.

"Tell me. Say it."

"My brother is dead. He's not coming back." The tears spill over. I loosen my grip and use both my thumbs to wipe her cheeks. "I know survivor's guilt is real. But I don't know what to do with it."

"Neither do I, but you can still tell me what you want. This can be shitty and hard and you can still tell me."

"I want you to hurt me. I want you to degrade me. I want you to turn me into a nothing little slut and then build me back up again. I want to feel something that isn't *this* for as long as possible. I need something to break. I need something in me to finally shatter. I couldn't get myself there at home and everyone around me was all about me pushing forward, but you can give me this. I know you can. It still doesn't make it okay for me to ask you to do it."

I know this is bad for both of us. For all the reasons she stated and because I know I can't trust my own feelings for her. They've already climbed to unsafe levels. But I have to give her what she wants. Fuck what the better part of my brain is telling me.

"Don't move."

I go over to my crate filled with random shit I haven't found a specific place for, grab a bungee cord that I haven't needed in a few months, then dig out a pair of scissors from my kitchen drawer. I walk back over to Claudia and spin her around and bind her hands behind her back with the cord. It has enough give so she can move, but not enough for her to get free. I grab the scissors.

"You wearing anything under this?"

"Just a bra." Her voice is shaking.

"Hope you're not too attached to this sweater. Or the bra."

"Wha—"

I grip the bottom of her sweater, pull it away from her body and start cutting from the bottom. The knit looks durable but it comes apart instantly under the blade.

I pull the open side apart and reach for the center of her bra.

"Wait!"

It's too late. I pull the center of her bra forward and cut it open too.

"Jesus, Shep."

"You'll recover. I swear. Turn around and bend over." Her feet are still free, but it's clear she's not used to being bound at all. She awkwardly turns around and then manages to bend over the edge of the counter. She makes a little noise when I grip the crotch of her stretchy pants and cut a small hole.

"Good thing I didn't like any part of this outfit."

"Less talking," I say. I toss the scissors on the counter and squat down behind her and rip her pants open at the seam. She has underwear on underneath that I shove to the side. She's wet. I toy with her a bit, sliding my finger up and down her slit. Then I stand and leave her there. I cross the room and make myself comfortable on the couch, adjusting my cock in my jeans as I sit.

"Now. I want you to turn around and get on your knees. Take your time."

She turns slowly again. She's pissed, but I don't care. She slowly sinks to her knees and I try not to laugh when it becomes apparent that I can only see the top of her head over the island counter.

"I hope you're happy," she says.

"You need to learn to understand your own demands. I want you to come over here. On your knees."

"I'm going to make you regret this," she grunts, but I see her head start bobbing around the edge of the counter. Titus trots over to see what the hell she's doing. I snap my fingers and order Titus over to his dog bed. He tries to lick Claudia's face for good measure before she ducks out of the way. I snap again.

"Go on, buddy. Leave Claudia alone." He finally listens and goes to sit down.

"Thanks."

"As soon as you get over here we can really have some fun. You can hurry up or you can keep running your mouth."

"I'm gonna bite you when I get over there."

"I can gag you right now if you want."

She stares at me, eyes narrowing as she shuffles forward, but she's making decent progress. I pull out my cock as she makes her way over and start to stroke myself. I don't miss the way she licks her lips. Finally she makes it over to the couch. She sits back on her heels, taking the pressure off her knees.

"What next, Master?"

"I told you Sir or Shep works just fine, but we can go with Master if you want to be a smartass. I can still dominate you even if you talk back. It's not bothering me one bit."

She sighs and cocks her head to the side. "What will you have me do next, Master?"

"Sit on my cock. Actually, fuck. Wait." I stand, tuck my hard on away, and snatch her off the floor. She screams as I toss her over my shoulder with ease and carry her into the bedroom. I set her upright and chuckle a little at the way her hair is all over her face. "Where are all those condoms you always carry with you?"

"Pink makeup case in my black bag—right there." I grab the little pouch and see that it's filled with condoms, enough to get us through the weekend. I shove two in my pocket.

"Great. Up you go."

"Oh fuck you, Shep," she screeches as I toss her over my shoulder again. I do laugh this time, but I straighten my expression by the time I set her back on the floor.

"Back on your knees," I say. I flop back down on the couch and open my pants. The tip of my dick is already leaking when I pull it out again. Claudia's breathing hard, but I'm not about to give her a break.

"Come on, it's not gonna suck itself."

"Are you sure?" she says. Still she comes forward.

"We could wait and see, but I'm not sure how that would work out for you."

"I thought you were so sweet an hour ago."

"Funny how things can change so fast. Suck it now."

She growls at me, still she leans over my lap and takes the head of my cock into her mouth. I hold back a groan. The wet heat just behind her lips feels fucking amazing. She pulls back a bit and I stroke my hand up, forcing a thick drop of precum from the tip. I look down at her staring up at me with homicide in her eyes but then she's licking the slit of my cock.

I grip the back of her head and gently push it down. She doesn't fight it. After a few bobs of her head she moans. She sucks me good, swirling her tongue around. I know I'm going to come in her mouth soon if I don't stop her.

"Enough of that. Get up here." I pull her by the hair, but she won't relinquish my cock so easily. She fights against my grip, dipping her head back down and rubbing her tongue all over the underside of my cock.

"Fuck. That's enough." I haul her up and pull her over my lap so she's straddling my dick. I pull out one of the condoms and quickly slide it on.

"There you go. Neatly wrapped. Have a seat."

"No."

"Excuse me."

"No," she says and then she shrugs. "I changed my mind. I don't really feel like it anymore."

"Oh is that right?"

"Yeah. I mean I'm sure you have some great board game—" I cut her off with one firm hand on her hip and the other on the base of my cock. I find her entrance with ease and slam home. "Shit," she whines. I rock my hips up and back, grab her other hip and pull her down even harder. "Shit," she says again.

"Uh huh. You were saying?"

"Shep."

"You still want to play board games?" I say.

"Yes. I wanna to beat your ass at Scrabble."

"Uh huh. Tell me more." I slide to the edge of the couch, then gather her hair in my right hand again. I'm guiding her hips with ease with my left. "Tell me what you want to do."

"Ah! Shep, fuck!"

"Keep going. I want to hear all about it. How you'd rather be looking at me with a board game between us than bouncing on my cock." I lean forward and take one of her tits in my mouth. I bite the tip. She makes a little hissing noise. I smooth the little mark I know I've made with the pad of my tongue and then I start to suck. She's whining now, arching against me. I don't even have to guide her hips anymore. She's riding the fuck out of my dick. I pull her head back and move my mouth up the side of her neck. I bite her some more. I suck. She's calling my name.

"None of that Shep shit. You didn't want me a few minutes ago. Tell me about all the other places you'd rather be right now," I tug a little harder on her hair and bring her lips to mine. "I want to hear you say it. I want to hear you say you don't want to be with me. Say it."

"I can't," she whimpers.

"Why not."

"Because I do," she cries. "I want to be with you."

"A little louder. I couldn't quite hear you."

"I want to be with you, Shep."

"Damn straight," I say and then I kiss her. She kisses me back, pressing her lips hard against mine. She can barely move her head, my grip on her hair is too strong. That doesn't stop her from slipping her tongue into my mouth. She's going wild now, grinding harder and harder against my lap. I want to nut. Her pussy is working me so good. She's so wet and so warm. So fucking tight, but I'm going to hold out.

She lets out this deep noise. It comes from deep in her chest and then she's coming on my cock. I want to follow her, let loose. Not yet. I lean back against the couch and pull her with me. I hold her against my chest. I start pumping my hips up and down. She's rubbing her cheek against my beard. She's begging. I reach down and spread her ass, gather up the wetness from her cunt that's spread all around and push one slick finger into her tightest hole.

"Shep," she moans. She comes again.

I lose it then, fucking her harder than I'm sure she'd been fucked in a while. She's limp against me, but I can still feel every muscle in her cunt working along my shaft.

"I'm coming," she says.

"I know, baby. I know. Come again. Come for me."

She does. I don't think I'll ever be able to tell her how good her pussy feels.

I want to torture us both a bit longer, but I remind myself of her bound hands and how long she was on her knees. And we have the rest of the night. The rest of the weekend. A whole week. I think about what it would be like with no barrier between us. I think about what I really want to tell her and I come, swearing against her lips before I kiss her.

A little while later, after we're both cleaned up and I've stripped her completely naked, I give her some water and burrito her in a blanket.

"What else do you have in mind tonight?" she asks. I've grabbed my laptop and she's leaning up against my side on the couch.

"Still have to shop. And I need to replace your sweater and your bra."

"And my leggings. Jerk. I loved those leggings."

"Do you regret it?"

"No," she pouts. "Your dick is magic. I just hate you for it."

I smile and shake my head. I look down at her when she sighs and wiggles so her head is on my thigh. I slide my left hand down her side and keep typing. I need to get some proper rope.

"We're just gonna keep doing this, aren't we?" she says. "I'm gonna remember that I have actual problems that I actually have to work on. I freak out. You make everything better. Tell me I should leave now, Shep." She looks up at me. I look down at her and then tilt her chin up. I kiss her.

"No."

CHAPTER ELEVEN

I remember to set my alarm a few minutes earlier than usual. Even Titus knows something's up when I reach over and shut it off. He cracks an eyelid at the foot of the bed and looks at me as I reach over to Claudia.

"Hey. Claudia." She wakes with a start and I have to move back before I catch an elbow to the face. "Hey, it's just me."

"Oh, god. Sorry." She closes her eyes and lets out a few stuttered breaths. "Hey what's up?"

"I'm going to take Titus out. I want you to come. It's still dark out though. You okay with that?"

"You're not going to leave me in the woods are you?"

"No. I promise."

"Okay. Yeah." She presses her face back into the pillow for a few seconds and then rolls over and shuffles to the other side of the bed.

The rest of our night is quiet. I put on a movie where Tom Cruise fights aliens with Emily Blunt. Claudia offers her opinion on every item I pick out online, from my preferred brand of condoms to the three dildos of varying lengths and girths I assure her will be inserted into all of her holes at my pleasure. She turns her nose up at the idea of a ball gag, but she's into the idea of massage oil, fishnet body suits, and garter belts and stockings. She knows we're going to have a good time.

After, she dozes with her head still in my lap and my hands idly play with her tits under the blanket. When I take her to bed, she wakes up and tells me she wants to make out. Her exact words. I kiss her until she reaches between my legs and starts stroking my cock. I fuck her to sleep.

She looks just as beautiful first thing in the morning as she does freshly fucked. She looks at me over her shoulder. She catches me looking at her bare back.

"I don't have proper hiking boots. Is that okay?"

"We'll stick to the trails. It'll be fine."

"Great," she groans and then she starts digging through her suitcase. I start to dress and laugh to myself as Titus finally perks up. He knows he's getting his walk in early. We're both ready in ten minutes or so. Claudia looks half dead like she's not fully awake, but still sexy as hell. Titus is ready to go. He's doing his panic dance by the front door.

"You want coffee?" I ask as she slips on her coat. I watch her as she pulls her hair up into a ponytail.

"No. I'm going back to sleep when we get back."

"Are you?"

"Uh yeah. You can boss me around all you want, but I'm pretty sure this whole domination submission thing works a lot better when one of us isn't yawning. Besides, it's Saturday, isn't it?"

"It is."

"There. We can spend the day napping and fucking. It'll be amazing. You ready?"

"Almost." I grab Titus's leash and then I get my shotgun.

"Do you take that every time you go out?" she asks.

"Only if I'm leaving my property. It's not for humans. It's for mountain lions and bears. Years ago they'd all be settled in for the winter by now, but now—"

"Fucking climate change. Okay well, let's hope we don't run into any bears." She pulls a pair of gloves out of her pocket and puts them on.

"You ever seen one in real life?" I ask.

I open the front door and Titus bolts down the steps and down the driveway. Claudia looks between us as I hand her the leash. I lock the front door, then I turn and take her gloved hand.

"No, I haven't and I'd like to keep it that way. We need the dog right? He didn't just take off for Vegas did he?"

I chuckle at how wide her eyes are. "He knows the routine. Come on." I lead her off the porch and around the north side of the house to the mouth of the trail at the rear of my property.

"Uh. So. Can you see in the dark 'cause...I don't see a flashlight or handy cellphone light in your other hand," she says once we clear the reach of my security lights.

"I know where I'm going and if you wait a minute you'll see it's not pitch black out here. There's a difference between dark and zero visibility."

"What in sweet nature man hell?"

I laugh. "Just relax and hold onto my hand."

"Oh I'm not letting go for sure. You can believe that."

I laugh again then slip my fingers into my mouth and let out a wolf whistle. It takes a few moments, but I can hear Titus's tags jiggling as he sprints around the side of the house. He slams into the side of my leg. I grab his collar and take the end of the leash from Claudia and clip it on, then hand it back to her.

"Think you can handle him?"

"Yeah, Mr. Grylls. You just keep your eye out for woodland creatures who want to eat me and I'll handle the pupper. I'm too cute to be mauled."

"I promise. You'll be safe. Come on." I lead her down the trail, holding the conversation until we get to the clearing. Claudia's not much for silence, but I can tell by the way she's gripping my hand she might be too afraid to talk. I ask her if she's okay and she quietly replies with a yes. After about a mile, the sky above us is already starting to grow brighter through the trees. There's still another hundred yards through the forest before we reach our destination, but the small gasp she lets out tells me she sees exactly what I see. The break in the trees and the wooded valley beyond.

I stop when we reach the clearing and take Titus's leash from Claudia's hand.

"Shep," she says quietly.

"Nice, huh?"

"Nice my ass. It's amazing. I think—I think this is what Miles wanted to show me. We just didn't get this far."

"I think he might have been taking you up to Grafton's Notch. That has a different view. You can only get this if you come from my property."

"It's really amazing. And we can watch the sunrise from here?"

"Mhmm. You want to have a seat?" I say as I nod over to a boulder a few dozen yards off the trail that has a natural ledge cut into its facade.

"Yeah." I let her lead the way. The rock is wider than it is tall and the ledge itself isn't that high off the ground. She hops up with ease and takes Titus's leash from me so I can set my gun before I climb up.

"I think we need more of a concrete plan to take some of the stress off you," I say once we're settled.

"Okay. Let's hear this plan."

"I'm not going to ask you to leave. I don't want you to. So let's just shelve that idea for the rest of your time here."

She lets out a deep breath that turns into a sigh. "Okay. I can do that."

"And I think we need to talk about what happened. I might not be a medical professional, but I do care about you and I do consider you to be a friend even if we're still getting to know each other. You can talk to me."

"I appreciate that and I guess you're right. For a long time I felt like you might be the only person I could talk to about it."

"You can, but I think we should balance it out with something else. I came up with a list of positive ice breaker questions," I say as I pull out my phone.

"You wrote a list on your phone?"

"Uh yeah. I like to be prepared for this sort of thing. It's what every good Dom and friend does."

Claudia's laugh echoes across the valley. She only scares a couple birds. "Shit. Sorry," she mutters. She looks adorable as fuck the way she ducks her head and covers her mouth. "Go on with your list."

"Okay and I will answer in kind so you're not just out here pouring out all this information."

"I appreciate it."

"Question one. What is your full name?"

"Oh the basics? Claudia Deja Cade."

"Shepard Nils Olsen. Nice to meet you."

She giggles again. "Likewise."

"When's your birthday? You mentioned you're a Gemini."

"June fifth. And you?"

"February fourteenth." I look over at her and she's looking back at me with her mouth hanging open. "Just say whatever you're going to say. Get it out of your system."

"You're just…so cranky. I want to envision this sweet Valentine's Day baby, but I can just picture you walking out of your mom with a full beard and that scowl on your face."

"And I punched the doctor to make him cry and stole my dad's cigar?"

Another hysterical laugh bursts out of her. "Yes, actually."

"I'm not cranky. Just accustomed to a certain way of living. People up here aren't much for light conversation and small talk."

"Well good thing we're sticking to hard hitting facts. What's next on your list, Dr. Love?"

"My grandfather used to call me Saint. Like Saint Valentine."

"That's so cute."

"I didn't want the other kids in my elementary school to know my birthday was Valentine's Day because I didn't want the attention, but my third grade teacher heard my grandfather call me Saint one day and it reminded her of my birthdate so she went all out. I was so pissed."

"I'm sorry. You're not going to get me to think of that as anything other than adorable."

"Moving on. What is your favorite breakfast food?"

"Oh that's tough. I like pretty much all breakfast food. Actually that's not true. I have a weird aversion to sausage links. I don't know, just give me a traditional breakfast platter. Some sort of carbs I can smother in butter and syrup. Roasted potatoes, not hash browns. Bacon. So much bacon. I'm a hipster t-shirt cliché. I love bacon. And cinnamon toast and hot chocolate. My dad used to make that for me when my mom wasn't home. So good."

"My grandfather used to make this super thick Norwegian porridge that his mother used to make him, rømmegraut. He didn't have a TV before I moved in with him, but my mom made him buy a TV and a VCR. On Saturday mornings he'd make it for me and we'd watch a video he would check out from the library." I know she can hear how raw my throat is getting. The exact reason I don't like to talk about him.

"I'm sorry he passed away, Shep."

"Thank you. I miss him. Cancer is a bitch." I'm a little shocked when she reaches down and takes my hand and even more shocked when she slips off the rock and comes to stand in front of me. She moves closer, then hands me Titus's leash and slips her arms around my waist.

"You think you're going to get out of talking by hugging me?" I ask her.

I feel her shaking with laughter before she pulls away a little. She looks at me a moment then tugs on my beard. "I miss Miles, but I miss my mom so much. Grenada is a small island, ya know. And we lived close to the water so it didn't take long to walk down to the beach. When we were little, my parents would take turns doing things with us individually. My mom would take me with her to run her errands, but she'd always work in something fun for us to do when we were out and about. My favorite days were when we would stop by the water and she would let me 'chase the waves'." I smirk at the little air quotes she uses.

"When we moved to the States, we didn't have any family here. We didn't know anyone and it was fucking freezing. The day before my first day of school she took me to the beach at Coney Island. I was all bundled up in my new winter coat and mittens and shit, but she told me to go chase the waves. I felt like an idiot at first. I'm running toward the water in a damn snowsuit, but I just remember turning around and seeing the look on her face. She didn't want to leave Grenada either, but she was happy because *I* was smiling again."

"When did they pass away?" I ask.

"About seven years ago. It was like your standard, run of the mill car accident. Nothing crazy, like an attempted double homicide, but it felt like they were literally stolen from us. It completely turned Miles around. He'd been fighting my dad on med school for years and then right after their funeral he got his shit together and applied. And I joined a grief support group. That's how I met my friend Liz and her sister. The group was bullshit, but I got two friends out of it, so whatever."

"Fair enough."

"I have this weird—sometimes I have these weird thoughts where I actually envy Miles. He gets to be with them again."

I reach up and cup the side of her neck. "That's not weird. You miss your family and you want to be with them again. I feel the same way most of the time."

"This would be a lot easier if it didn't feel so shitty."

"I'm sure it would be." I lean forward and kiss her. "Turn around."

She turns and I move a little closer to the edge of the boulder and wrap my arms around her shoulders. She takes my hand and rubs her lips across my knuckles. We watch the sun come up.

I make her eggs and bacon and carbs she can smother in butter and syrup. She's tickled to see I still use my grandfather's griddle top that he'd picked up sometime during Kennedy's administration. She wins the argument about the nap. We nap. Titus decides he's sick of our bullshit and wedges himself between us on the bed. Claudia wakes me up because she wants more food.

It's my turn to be confused. No one's woken me up in a while. She tells me she's hungry. I tell her she's high maintenance and she needs to get the fuck out of my house as I pull out some of the food May-Bell dropped off. We eat on the couch and she makes me watch the first season of a spin-off show based on another show that's based on a book. It's fucking terrible and I can't even pretend to be interested, so I slip to the floor between her legs and see if I can test her concentration. The night before I was distracted by the moment. Now I take my time. She actually tries to ignore me.

"Babe. Move that big ass, hairy head of yours a little to the left. But keep doing what you're doing."

I grab the remote and turn off the TV. "That's the end of that."

"Hey! They get married in that episode."

"And you're about to get fucked in this episode. Up, and bend over the couch."

"What. Ever. You. Are. The. Worst." She stands and stomps her feet as she strips down naked.

"Yeah, I'm not interesting in your bratty showboating. Over the couch, slut," I add for a little flavor.

She gasps and flips her ponytail over her shoulder. "Well I never." Then she bends over and uses both her hand to spread her cheeks. "You are *so* rude."

I shake my head even though she can't see me. I pull a condom out of my pocket and hold it between my teeth as I strip naked. "Keep those cheeks open." Once I slip the condom on I take my time teasing her. I can't believe how wet she gets. I tell her.

"It's 'cause I'm such a slut, Master Shep. I'm always wet for you."

"Always talking so much shit." She laughs, but I turn that chuckle of hers right into a moan as I slide my cock inside her tight slit. I push in and out a few times, then slap her hands away. She braces herself on the back of the couch.

"You were fucking up my leverage," I say. She laughs some more, but she can barely catch her breath. I pick up my pace. This is why I can't stand regular sex. I like the anticipation. I like drawing things out. The suffering, the begging. I like to see my submissive driven crazy by the need to come before I even get started. But Claudia, fuck, her pussy feels so good and the sight of her ass as it bounces against my hips. I reach forward and slide my hand up over her tits. I pinch her nipples.

"Wait, Shep. Shep! Stop."

I freeze. "Did I hurt you?"

"No. Do you hear that?" I hear it, but before I realize I'm hearing footsteps outside my front door, there's a loud knock.

"The fuck," I say under my breath.

"Know you're home, Shepard. It's Jad!"

"Ah, fuck. Not a good time, Jad!"

"Who the fuck is Jad?" Claudia asks.

"May-Bell's husband."

He knocks again. He knocks louder. I know Jad is getting on in years, but now he's just fucking with me. "Hold on! Sorry, baby." I pull out and nudge her over on the couch cushions. She groans and shoves her hand between her legs.

"Here. Hide." I toss a blanket on top of her and go crack the front door open. It's fucking freezing, and the air feels like it's about to snow and there's Jad standing on my porch.

"Afternoon, Jad. This is a really bad time. A little occupied at the moment."

He can only see my face and about half of my shoulder, but he still looks me up and down. He makes a face. "I thought she was just visiting."

"Jad. Please."

"There's a tree down over at our place and my chainsaw is busted. I need to borrow yours."

I'm tempted to chuck the keys to my shed at Jad's head, but he helped raise me and he knows I was raised with better manners than that. He's also a man of the mountain who's almost my size. I've never tested him before, but I'm not sure he can't take me.

"One second." I try to close the door, but he walks right in. "Christ, Jad."

"Oh I've seen your bare ass before, boy. Hurry up." It's not my ass I'm worried about. It's my half deflated cock and the condom I'm still wearing. And the naked woman on my couch.

I grab my pants off the floor and dig up my shirt. I do something I've never wanted to do and pull the condom off and shove it in my pocket. It takes me a second to find my keys on the table, then stomp into my boots. "Come on. It's out in the shed."

He follows me outside, but I catch him trying to look around me to get a glimpse of the couch.

"Did you really come by for the chainsaw?" I ask once we're outside.

"I did, you smartass. Unlike my wife, I don't need to pry into your business. You've got a lady in there, you got a lady in there. It's good. Glad your pecker's working and I was little worried you'd gone insane after the thing with Sarah."

"Don't need to talk about her, Jad. It's been a while, but I'm fine."

"Yeah. That's what Egil used to say."

I unlock the shed door and grab my chainsaw off the shelf.

"Thank you." Jad reaches for it, but I shake my head.

"I got it." We walk down the driveway and I set it in the bed of his truck. "Hold on to that as long as you want."

"I'm gonna replace mine next week. Just needed something in a hurry." He turns to me with his hands on his hips. "Bring her on by tonight. May-Bell's cooking. Like always. You two come by."

"Alrighty."

"People love you, Shepard. I know it's a hardship. We just want to meet the woman *you* love."

"Whoa. Who said anything about that?"

Jad's eyebrow goes up. "Just like Egil. Dinner's at seven. We'll see you then."

Jad gets in his truck and I stand there and wait until he's back down the drive and headed on his way. I squeeze my eyes shut for a second before I head back inside. Claudia is sitting up on the couch wrapped in the blanket when I walk through the door.

"Is the coast clear?" she asks.

"Yeah, he's gone."

"Great." She stands and tosses the blanket off. "Where were we?"

I laugh a little at the huge smile on her face. "Give me a second. Conversations with Jad are a bit of a boner killer."

Her expression drops. "What did he say?"

"Nothing. He just invited us over for dinner tonight."

"Oh." She sounds about as excited as I am. "Are we going?"

"We're going."

"But you don't want to."

"I can think of better ways to spend a Saturday night. With you."

"And we can't get out of this?"

"No." I pull off my shirt and head back into my bedroom to grab another condom. Claudia dumped them out on my shelf so I don't have to keep asking where she's keeping her little pink pouch thing. I drop my pants and start stroking myself. "They will come back. Both of them."

"Let me help you with this and then we'll go and have dinner with your very interesting neighbors." She scoots to the edge of the couch and opens her mouth.

"Thanks. You're really looking out for number one right now."

"I know. Me. I want sex. In. Now." She points to her lips. I walk over and slide right in. I should probably warn her about how intense May-Bell and Jad can be, but that'll have to wait until later. Claudia's mouth feels too good.

CHAPTER TWELVE

Jad's surprise visit almost fucks up my whole afternoon, but Claudia helps me get back on track. I fuck her until I can't stand anymore. She comes on my cock a few times, begging me not to stop even though she can barely lift her head. After we catch our breath she gets in the shower and comes back to the great room wearing the red long john one-piece pajamas Sarah got me one year as a gag gift. I never even tried them on, but they look a shitload better on Claudia than they would have on me, especially since she hasn't buttoned the top all the way and her perfect tits are hanging out.

I ask her where she found them. She casually says she found them in my closet. I want to ask her what she was doing in my closet, but she starts telling me that she's my guest and it was "super" rude of me to interrupt her in the middle of her streaming television program. She flops back down on the couch and grabs the remote. I give her a minute to get comfortable. I pull on my pants and check Titus's food and water situation. Then I stroll back over to the couch and sweep Claudia up into my arms.

She screeches but doesn't try to fight me when I pick her up and fall on top of her on the couch. I tickle her, bite at her neck and tits until she's wheezing from laughter and then I kiss her until I feel myself hitting that point. I need to pull back. I swing us both upright and pull her into my lap and watch three episodes of this weird ass show with her.

She has the nerve to say she would make the perfect vampire and I tell her she clearly isn't patient enough for immortality and that launches us into a whole discussion about how she's pretty sure I'm actually a werewolf and my remote mountain home is all just an elaborate cover. She's pretty deep into how she thinks Titus is actually my cousin who can't change back to his human form when I realize how much I like listening to her talk about this kind of nonsensical shit. I can listen to her talk about just about anything.

We call it quits on the paranormal primetime drama when she tells me she needs at least an hour to get ready for a formal dinner. I remind her that it isn't formal and she tells me to mind my business when it comes to her business. She indirectly shames me into putting on a decent shirt and running a comb through my hair even though I put my hat right back on.

She takes more than an hour to get ready. I give her shit for it when she comes out of my bedroom, but not before I look her up and down. She's wearing another pair of skin tight jeans and different pair of tan boots that come up to her thighs. She has on a long sleeved sweater that's dark red and makes her tits look almost obscene. She's put on makeup. I realize she hasn't been wearing much or any since she got here. She doesn't need it, but she looks amazing.

"Took you fucking long enough," I say as I stand. I want to cancel this stupid dinner and spend the rest of the night worshipping her body on my own dining room table.

She fluffs her hair out and puts a hand on her hip. "Phsst whatever, bitch. You cannot rush perfection and you know I look good."

I walk over to her and pull her into my arms. "You look amazing."

"I would be a jerk and say something smart about how you're not that cute, but you're sexy as hell and I want you to do all kinds of things to me right now."

"When we get back. I'll do things."

"What kind of things?"

"Kind of fucked up things."

"I like that." She lightly kisses me on the lips. I can still smell that pineapple but she's added something glossy and sticky. "Sorry," she laughs when she catches me wiping my mouth. "I'll make sure I take it off when we do the kinda fucked up things later tonight."

I grab her ass and nudge her toward the door. "If you're good. Come on, T!" Titus comes sprinting out of the kitchen and joins us as we head out to the truck. I have to wrestle him into the back of the cab, but he's still happy to be coming along.

"Okay. Is there anything I need to know before I go into this lion's den?" Claudia asks when we pull back out to the main road.

"It's not much of a lion's den. It's just The Tierneys. Jad and May-Bell will both try to grill you in their own way. Just be upfront. That's the only advice I can give you. Jad is a walking lie detector. He used to be the county sheriff, and May-Bell is just nosy as hell. Tell them what they want to know in the simplest terms up front and they'll get off your back and move on to something else."

"So don't tell them how I'm an ex-Las Vegas showgirl turned investigative reporter turned treasure hunter who heard there was gold up in these hills?"

"You can certainly try that. They might ask me if there's something really fucking wrong with you. I think the truth will work."

"Fine." She sighs.

When we pull up to May-Bell and Jad's I'm glad to see that Jad wasn't bullshitting about needing my chainsaw. One of the pines in their yard went over and luckily missed the roof. It's in freshly cut pieces up against the side of the house and there's sawdust and wood chips all over the place.

I pull up behind May-Bell's SUV and turn to Claudia. "Ready?"

"Is this the closest I'll ever get to meeting your parents?"

"Yes," I said. No need to bullshit her. Even if we did something nuts like get married, she'd never meet my real parents.

"Okay." She lets out a deep breath. "Let's do this."

We survive introductions. May-Bell, always the proper hostess, places dinner on the table and Jad offers us our choice of beers from his two favorite kinds of ale. May-Bell seats me across from Claudia. I don't like it, but Claudia seems comfortable when she takes her seat. She smiles and winks at me.

"Claudia, honey, you ever had venison stew? It's Shep's favorite," May-Bell sáys.

"No I haven't, but it smells delicious. Thank you so much." She passes her bowl and lets May-Bell serve her a healthy portion.

"I made a tart too. Jad's watching his sugar so you can take the rest of it back over to Shep's with you tonight."

"That's so kind. Thank you," Claudia says.

"So tell us a little bit about yourself, Claudia. Where ya from?" Jad asks.

"Um, New York. I live in Manhattan."

"Oh, quite the difference from our small mountain town. How do you like it out here so far?"

"I actually haven't gotten to see much of the town yet, but the people down at the Light Grass Lodges were great and Connie?"

"Oh yeah, Connie's a good friend of mine."

"She's underselling it. Connie's her BFF. They text each other all day long," I say. May-Bell frowns at me.

"My uh—my brother and I didn't explore the town much last time I was here," Claudia says. "But I would like to see more of it. I've been by the diner a couple times and Connie was very sweet to me."

"She knows how to do service with a smile. It's how we say welcome around here." I almost roll my eyes. May-Bell is laying it on a little thick.

"Well we're glad you're back, after your brother passed," Jad says. He realizes his fuck up immediately and looks up, his eyes darting between me and Claudia. "'Pologies. I didn't mean to bring it up that way."

"It's okay. Really. It's not something that can't be taken back and it's kind of the reason I'm here now."

"Not many people would send a thank-you note, but I saw Jerry—Sheriff Bingham—this morning and he said it was nice to see you again. We're all glad you made it out alive. We're glad Shep was there," Jad says.

"Jad," May-Bell warns.

"No, it's okay. It was…a bad situation. A thank-you note didn't seem sufficient. I'm just glad I'm alive to say thank you. Especially to Shep," Claudia says.

"What do you do in New York City?" May-Bell asks.

"Um, I'm actually in between jobs right now. I was a buyer in women's apparel for Kleinman's, but I resigned about a month ago. I'll be looking for the next gig soon."

"Oh what happened? Why'd you resign?" May-Bell asks.

"Just wasn't the right fit anymore, but we'll see what else is out there."

"You looking around here?" Jad asks. "I heard they are still looking for a new children's librarian back in town."

"Oh no, I—I'm just visiting. I have to head back at the end of the week."

I'm fine with this answer. This answer is in line with my expectations. I know she's going. This isn't a shock or a surprise to me, but Jad responds with another one of his meaningful looks. I can feel the cloud passing over my own face as I stare back at him. I know he has more sense than to go there, but he can't help himself.

"Well nice of Shep to give you someplace to stay while you're in town."

"I invited her to stay with me," I say. "Didn't make much sense for her to pay to stay at the Lodges when there are perfectly good accommodations right up here."

"Mhmm. How long are you staying?"

"Just until Friday?"

"Well hopefully you get back to see us. Shep hasn't had many visitors in a while."

I sigh and put down my fork. "She knows Jad."

Jad's nails me with a look. "Does she know how long it's been since you've had visitors? Does she know why?"

"Yes. She knows. She knows about Sarah and she knows I'm an anti-social prick."

"Does she know Sarah's the one who took care of her during the day shift?" He looks at Claudia who has now gone a little pale. "Did he tell you about the trips he takes so he can get over her?"

"Jad. Enough," May-Bell's voice is calm, but deadly. It's enough to shut Jad up, but only for a minute. He's been holding this shit in for years, but we can't do this now. Not in front of Claudia. And it's also none of Jad's business.

"May, thank you for a lovely dinner," I say as I start to stand. My chest is pounding and I can hear water rushing in my ears, but I have to keep it together long enough to get Claudia and Titus back to the house. Then I can channel this shit somewhere else.

"Shepard, sit down," Jad says. The authority in his voice makes me want to punch him clean in his throat. He doesn't run this mountain anymore.

I keep standing, but I don't leave. I know what I have to say or else I might punch Jad. "You think I'm just as screwed up as Egil. You can say it. You think I'm just as screwed up as my mother. Probably worse, but I will never understand what you want from me, Jad. I'm fine. I'm employed. I'm taking care of my property and my dog. I'm not doing anything wrong.

"Sarah spreads my business all over this mountain, then splits with some other dude and somehow I'm the monster. You know Julia Tompkin's kid told me there's a rumor going around the high school that I kill women up at my place and Jerry protects me? I shared something about myself with the woman I loved almost three years ago and people were afraid to look at me. All it took was stopping a serial killer and finally people start treating me like a person again. But not quite. Right? I'm sorry if I invited a friend to stay at my place."

"But she's not your friend, Shep. She doesn't know you and you barely know her. No offense," he says to Claudia. I almost tell him not to speak to her but he barrels right through. "You two were thrown together by something terrible and months later she's back so you can shack up for a few days?"

"You're out of line, Jad. You know nothing about us. And even if you did, I'm allowed to have guests up to my house!"

Jad shoots out of his chair, but knows not to get in my face. "And no one says you're not! But you don't have guests over to your place and you haven't in years and I'm sorry if it raises a little concern when Claudia here is the first in some time. I told Egil it wasn't good for him to keep you up here that way. He used the mountain as an excuse after Letta passed and now—"

"And now what? Just say it, Jad. I turned out just like him, but worse because I'm some sort of danger to the delicate women of Paluma County."

"No. You deserve something healthy and happy and this is not how it starts. Again no offense, Claudia. But you can't keep doing this, Shepard and you know it."

I shake my head. I didn't come here to get Jad Tierney to understand anything about me or my life. I push my chair in and look over at Claudia. "Let's go."

Claudia stands and goes to grab our coats.

"Shep, please don't leave," May says.

"I'm sorry, May-Bell." I kiss her on the cheek, then snap for Titus. He's made himself comfortable by the fire with Fox, but he comes. He follows Claudia out to my truck and I do my best not to slam the door to their house behind me.

I take a deep breath when I climb behind the wheel.

"That wasn't about you," I say. "That was all about me and some of it was about my grandfather."

"It's okay, Shep. Really. Let's just go back to your place and watch a movie or something."

I don't say anything. I just start my truck and slowly back down the driveway.

We're quiet the rest of the way back. I'm too pissed to talk and I can't wrap my mind around the sheer size of the balls on Jad. I can't even contemplate what Claudia might be thinking. It's barely eight o'clock when we walk back in the door and I know Claudia only got to eat five or six bites of her dinner. I need to feed her and I need to get myself together so she doesn't have to spend the rest of the night worried about how pissed I really am.

I sit on the edge of the couch and scrub my face with both my hands. Claudia sits on the coffee table in front of me. She's quiet for a long time. I'm not trying to shut her out, but my chest is still tight. I need more time.

"I get it, Shep. Really." She reaches forward and I let her take my hand. Titus takes that as a sign that he should come over and lick both our knuckles. Claudia smiles and scratches his head. "Thank you for the kisses, T," she coos. Then she sighs and looks back up at me. "They are just protective of you and my showing up here and staying with you this way looks shady as fuck."

"It's not that. They think...everything that happened with my mom and my grandfather made me the way I am."

"So what's the truth? You tell me. What made you the way you are?"

"I don't know if you're born an introvert or not, but I'm an introvert and so was my grandfather. My grandma and Sarah brought us out of our shells."

"And they think a love lost made you both crazy hermits instead of just sending you back to your introverted ways."

"Pretty much. I know my grandfather could have tried to remarry, but he didn't. He focused on me and I won't lie and say I'm not grateful for that."

"You're grandfather sounds like he was a pretty great man. His name was Egil?"

"Yeah."

"That's a bad ass fucking name."

"He was pretty bad ass. He was a park ranger and being up here alone suited him just fine. People thought he was all mad and broken, but—"

"He was just minding his own business."

"Yes."

She nods and rubs her fingertips over my knuckles. I look at her dark nail polish. "That's the nice thing about living in the city. Millions of people minding their own damn business. It's lovely. So where does the other stuff come from? The kinky stuff."

I sigh and just give her the dull truth. "The internet. Then college. Then people I met when I would go to the city for the weekends. Same way anyone figures out what they're into."

"Damn."

"What?"

"I was hoping for something way crazier."

"Sorry to disappoint."

"Ask me some more questions from your list?"

I look at her for a moment. She's serious. I sit back and I pull out my phone. "What was your favorite movie growing up? What was your least favorite movie? Do you have any pets?"

"No pets. We had a dog named Coco when I was like six, but after she died my dad cried for like two weeks. My mom said no more pets. Favorite movie? I don't know. Too many to name." She cocks her head to the side and makes a clicking noise with her tongue. "Have you seen *Weekend At Bernie's*?"

That makes me laugh. "Yes. It was one of the classics we checked out from the library."

"Miles loved that stupid movie and I *hated* it. The man is decomposing. By the beach! He would have smelled so bad. Ugh. So gross."

I laugh and turn her hand over in my mine. "It was a pretty stupid movie."

"I don't think you're screwed up, Shep. Sarah sounds like a dick and if I'd known she was my day nurse I wouldn't have brought her flowers, but it sounds like she just didn't get you. Breakups are hard, but you obviously loved her and trusted her. She shouldn't have told people about your sex life. Especially in a town this small. Did she really think she was in danger with you?"

"I don't know. She wasn't."

"I don't think she was either. You're rough and cranky as fuck, you do snore, but you're a sweet, gentle man, Shep."

"I never hurt her. I think she was pissed at me for not being exactly what she wanted. She was pissed that I wasn't the full package. She texted me after she left town and told me she was still in love with me. She said that she would come back if I would just change."

"That's kind of shitty."

"It was. But it doesn't matter now. And Jad needs to get the fuck over it. You hungry?" She nods. "Are you above burgers?"

"Never."

I make us a simple dinner and we watch more of her vampire show. I had something in mind for after we got back from Jad and May-Bell's. It involved that bungee cord and some duct tape I found in the shed, but I know I'm too raw and still too pissed to do the scene right. A fuck up in the wrong headspace and I will hurt her. She says she's going to change for bed and we'll finish off the first season of Vampire Werewolf Bayou Blood Alliance.

That's what I'm calling it. I tell her to skip the pajamas and we both strip down to nothing.

I lay down on the couch and pull her whole body on top of mine. This is what I wanted the first night, every bit of her against me, skin to skin. I drape the blanket over us and spend the rest of the night running my hands up and down her bare back. My hands take periodic trips to her ass. I'm about to ask her what the fuck is going on with this teen witch girl when she tells me she is wet.

She lifts her head off my chest and looks me in the eyes. "Like really wet," she says. My cock's been behaving itself, but the moment she looks at me with those eyes my dick comes to life. I know she can feel it along her stomach. She squirms a little.

"You should see how wet I am," she says.

"You want me to check?"

She nods.

I slip my hands down and grab her fully by the ass, and pull her body up so we're face to face. I look down at her mouth and catch a glimpse of her tongue as it runs along the inside of her upper lip. I pull her ass cheeks apart with ease and I barely have to move my fingers an inch before I'm rubbing my hand in all this wetness. I'm a little shocked.

"When did this happen?" I ask.

She shrugs. "Last two hours or so."

"Oh really?"

"Yes. I was thinking about you and how nice it would feel to come just from rubbing my clit all over you."

I slide the tip of my middle finger just inside her pussy. She's soaking wet and perfectly hot. "I'm not sure if I know what you mean. You should probably show me."

"'Kay." She leans down and licks my bottom lip, then she slips her hands between our bodies and lines the hardness of my shaft up with her wet slit. She starts to move and then she kisses me.

CHAPTER THIRTEEN

CLAUDIA

I'm lost. So lost to this moment between us. I'm doing so many things wrong. For one, even though he hasn't even penetrated me yet, I know one of us needs to pause and grab a condom, but I can't stop myself from sliding my clit along his cock. I don't know how this feels for him, but he has no idea how good this feels for me. I know I shouldn't feel this way, especially after that awkward as fuck dinner with the Tierneys. They exposed Shep in the most brutally honest, yet the most cruel way. I know I should be taking stock. I should be thinking about stepping back, but I can't. I just want him more. I also want to go back down the hill and get those roses back from that nurse, Sarah.

Shep grips my ass harder and raises his hips. That feeling, when you know you're so close to coming, that electricity that shoots up your clit, makes you crazy, sends you chasing the sensation over and over, that's what I feel. I'm going to come. I rock against that friction. I move up a bit more so I can shove my tongue into his mouth. It's warm under the blanket and I can feel our sweat starting to slick my body. His mustache tickles my face, but I don't care. His tongue is so slick and dirty against mine.

I'm with Shep now, I keep telling myself. I'm with him and he's not going to ask me to leave. He's not going to tell me what we're doing is wrong. He's just as fucked up as I am, and in the back of my mind, I've started something I had no business starting. Something that's going to fuck us both up even more, like forever.

I can't decide whether or not I want to admit to Shep just how right he is. I want him. I want him all the time and he was right, I'm willing to beg for it. I can add that to the list of things I'll eventually have to discuss with a future therapist. It's not even the promise of sex that's driving me. It's his touch. It's the way he looks at me. Damn those deep brown eyes that seem to focus on me everywhere I turn. Damn that perfectly crafted beard. And that cock.

"I'm gonna come," I tell him, but before he can respond, say anything encouraging or nasty, I do come. I bury my face against his neck. He holds me closer, tries to hold me still, but my hips won't stop. I want more.

"That's it, baby," he says against my forehead and then he kisses my scar. Kisses all along it again and I come again. I'm shaking, but he's got me. He's still holding me to his chest, both his massive arms wrapped around me. Jason would never.

"You want me to come?" he asks me. Of course, I do, but I can barely speak. I just nod. "There's a condom in my pocket. Grab it." I groan in disappointment, but he slaps my ass. "Go on."

I use a surge of energy I can barely spare to toss off the blanket and make my shaky legs connect with the floor. I have to blink a few times before I can see properly but I find his jeans over by the TV. I'm ashamed and little disgusted at myself at the thought that crosses through my head as I dig the three condoms he has stashed from his back pocket. I don't want to use them. I want to be safe. I'm on the pill, but it only takes one hormonal slip up for the pill to be rendered useless—but I also want to know what it feels like.

I turn back to the couch and find Shep sitting up on the edge of the cushion. I hand him one of the condoms. He looks at me as he rips open the wrapper. I can't even think about looking away.

"You don't want me to use it," he says as he slips it on.

"Not in the stupid way though."

"Oh, I know," he says. He starts rubbing the palm of his hand over the swollen head of his cock. I swallow the drool that's pooling in my mouth. "Can you wait?"

I nod my yes and my thighs seem to squeeze together on their own. I've just come twice, but something about his voice and what he's suggesting has my clit aching again. He holds his hand out and I let him pull me close. He gathers me closer, bringing me down to straddle his lap. He grips his cock and pushes it inside me with shameful ease. He's so big, but I am so ready for him. I close my eyes and suck in a breath as I gently swirl my hips. I suck in another breath as he palms my breast and takes my nipple in his mouth.

"I'm too close and it's too risky," he says. The sound of his voice kills me. So deep and gravelly.

"I know" I sigh.

"But soon, I'll come all over you. Do you want that?" he asks.

"Yes," I reply.

"Soon. Make me come," he says. "Right now."

I take his cheeks in my hands and press my lips to his. I ride him hard, flexing and clenching my pussy. I ignore my own pleasure and focus on the sounds he's making, the groans, the harshness of his breath, the way he's grasping at my skin. He pulls away from me with a loud moan and a "Holy fuck!" and even though his cock is covered, I can feel him flexing inside me. I can feel everything. I don't want it to stop.

I wake up at four a.m. Another nightmare, but this time I don't scream. I just jerk myself awake. My heart isn't pounding, it's trying to claw its way out of my chest. I'm in an episode of that vampire show, but it's mixed with this movie I saw about terrorists taking hostages at an all boys boarding school and I'm there and I'm famous. More famous than I should be.

I've seen this episode before. I get shot in the back, but I survive. I try to retrace those steps, but none of the other actors are following the script. I have to hide somewhere else. I check all the halls and all the closets, and there's nowhere to go. I'm back in Kleinman's suddenly and I go to hide under a mountain of unfolded sweaters and jeans, but I'm moving too much and a gunman sees me. I wake up right when he pulls his trigger.

I can't breathe when I open my eyes. I feel the tears stinging at my lids, but I hold them back, thinking of how bad my chest hurts. Shep and Titus are both knocked out, both snoring. I look at Shep in the darkness. I want to wake him up. I want him to hold me, but he had a terrible night and managed to shove it all down to please me the way I wanted him to. He looks too peaceful to be disturbed.

I slip out of bed and dig up my phone. I quietly walk into his living room. It's so cold, in every way. I wrap myself in that blanket and I send a text to Liz. She might be awake.

I can't sleep.

What's wrong?
What did he do?
I'll kill him.

Nothing. I add a laughing emoji.
Just had a bad dream.

Oh, Laudi. I'm sorry.
Do you want me to call you?

Nah. Shep's still asleep
and it's quiet enough to hear a pin drop.

So? I'll call you anyway.
I'll tell him to fuck right off.
You come first.

Really you don't have to.
I just wanted to text you.

I want you to come home.
I'm worried about you.
I know he seems nice, but I'm still worried.

I know, but I'm okay. I promise.
Also, he's great. And I'll be back soon.
I just have to see this through.

What are you seeing through, exactly?

I don't know. I have no idea.

My throat tightens and I feel some fat tears gathering up weight in the corners of my eyes.

I don't want to cry ever again.
I need to figure that out.

That's a lofty goal, boo.
Promise me you'll take care of yourself
when you get back.
I want you to put you first.

I will.
I am.

In a healthy way. I'm not saying go back
to Kleinman's or even Dr. Dumbass.
Just, you know. Better.
You know I'm here for you
and so is Big Boobs Brook.

I laugh out loud alone in the dark. Liz's sister gave herself that nickname. It's always funny.

I know.

I glance up and see the outline of Shep standing in the bedroom door. I'm still rattled from my dream and the rawness of my text conversation with Liz, but my pulse cranks up even higher. "Jesus Christ," I gasp. "You scared the shit out of me."

"Sorry. I just wanted to come check on you. You okay?" he says. His voice sounds weird in the darkness. Weird to me, like it should be comforting, but something about it isn't quite hitting the mark. I know why. Because I'm about to lie to him.

"Yeah, I'm fine. I just had a nightmare. I didn't want to wake you up."

"You want to come back to bed? I don't have to take Titus out for a few more hours and it's freezing out here."

"Sure." I stand and text Liz back.

I'm going to try and get a little more sleep.

And then I cross the room. I don't realize I have the blanket wrapped around me still until Shep puts his arm around my shoulder. I expect a kiss or some rugged manly gesture. Shep seems to have a thing for picking me up. I'm relieved when he doesn't. I know what comes next if he does. He sweeps me up. He touches me. He kisses me. I beg him to fuck me. He does. But I don't have it in me right now.

I don't have the energy for the what comes next and the what comes after that. This is when Jason asks me a stupid question and I blow him to shut him up, but Shep kisses the top of my head and leads me over to the bed. He takes the blanket from me, then holds back the covers and waits for me. Titus huffs and moves around like we are disturbing the hell out of his peaceful slumber. Shep tells him to shut up and that makes me laugh a little. My phone vibrates in my hand.

Okay. Get some sleep. Love you!

Love you too.

I add five kissy face emojis. I set my phone on the floor as Shep climbs in on his side of the bed. He's spooning me before I can roll back over.

"I like being here with you," I tell him as I roll to face him. It's the truth, but I feel like I have to tell him because I'm holding so much else back.

He squeezes me tighter. "I'm trying not to let that go to my head," he says.

I want to tell him I love him. I don't know if I do, but I want to tell someone who isn't Liz or Brook something that matches what I'm feeling. That it hurts not to tell certain people I love them anymore, face to face. I open my mouth before I can stop myself.

"Can I tell you I love you even if I don't know if I mean it? I don't think I mean it, that way."

"With that caveat, yeah."

"I love you so much. It hurts." I say as I bury my nose in his chest hair. I'm crying again. His hand strokes down my back. He kisses the top of my head.

"I love you too."

*

Saturday was much heavier than we both want to admit. Sunday we decide to chill. He walks Titus without me. I'm conflicted about this when I wake up, like actually kind of pissed. I needed the sleep and I wasn't in the mood for an early morning walk through the woods, but I hate it when Shep leaves me in the house alone. I know he locks the doors and we're in the middle of nowhere, but still. I've been in the middle of nowhere before. But I did need the sleep. He's up making breakfast when I finally wake up and realize I desperately need a shower.

There's coffee when I get dressed. After we eat, Shep forces me to watch *First Blood*. I pretend to hate it, but I break down in a combination of hysterical tears and laughter when I admit that I used to make Miles watch it all the time when we were kids because he did the funniest impression of Sylvester Stallone.

Shep admits to me that his grandfather and Jad used to watch this movie together like it was Monday Night football. He also vows to find something I'll really hate for making him sit through almost a whole season of *The Originals*. I tell him if he digs up *Weekend at Bernie's* I'll burn down his house and steal his dog. He gets that I'm not joking.

We manage to keep our genitals apart all day, but I am horny as fuck by the time we finish doing the dinner dishes. I tell Shep that we need to do something about his jizzing all over me. I'm half joking, but he gets serious and sits me down on the island stools.

"I want to check in with you first and see if you're still interested in submitting to me this week." he asks.

"Yes. Of course I am. We've been fucking all weekend. Why? Do you have a new quest for me?"

He makes a face, but nods. "Yes."

Now I'm concerned. "What's up?"

"I've never been with anyone who talks back as much as you do, but I like it. I finally figured out a way to punish you that won't end up being a backhanded punishment for me. We took this weekend off, but I would like to start fresh tomorrow."

"We can do that."

"Do you understand what a safe word is and how it works?" I make a face, but he is dead serious and he's not budging. I cough and sit up.

"A safe word lets you know that I'm not cool with what's happening and I want you to stop."

"That's correct. I want you to pick a safe word."

"How about 'hedgehog'? I have no reason whatsoever to say that word."

"Hedgehog works just fine. Tomorrow you will be with me all day, including first thing in the morning when I go out to photograph the mountain so we're going to go to bed early. The post office will let me know when our stuff is here. We'll head down to town and pick that up and run some other errands. Probably have dinner down there and then we'll come back up and play for a little while. If you behave."

"Okay…" I'm dying to know what he means. "Will this be another tits out dinner?"

"Probably. Is that a problem?"

"No."

"Good. Go take off your clothes and go lie on the bed."

"Yes, sir," I say with a little two fingered salute. His eyes narrow at me as I hop off the stool. I laugh. "What? I'm following your directions."

"Mhmm."

I go into the bedroom and I find that I'm back in the mood by the time I'm naked on top of the bed spread. I look up when he walks into the room. The sight of him pulling off his shirt makes me swallow.

"Roll over," he says. I roll onto my stomach and wait, listening to the sound of him pulling off the rest of his clothes and then he's crawling over me. I love the heat from his body and feeling of his chest hair along my back. He kisses me all over, my cheeks, my shoulders, all the way down my back.

He moves me to my knees and his mouth is on my pussy. His licks every inch, kisses my lips open for him, sucks on my clit. His tongue pushes inside me. It feels so good. I tell him. I tell him not to stop, but he does. I whine and complain, but I know it's just getting started.

The next thing I feel is his hips pressing against my ass and his shaft rubbing along my slit. It's like the night before but it feels different. It feels better. He grips my hips and starts moving me back and forth, slowing until I'm moving on my own, driving myself crazy.

"That's right," he says. "Get me nice and wet." I lean forward a bit, spread my legs even more. My pussy is open, clenching for him. I can almost feel him entering me from behind, feel every inch, like a phantom sensation. All he has to do is shove his way in. I start to feel myself going over. Just a few more seconds and I know I'll come.

Shep stops my hips. He pulls away. I whine some more, but he tells me to be patient.

He slides back up the length of my body, moves his hand along my stomach then lower on my thigh to urge me to lay flat again. I feel his cock along my ass and then he's gathering my hair in his hand, bracing himself with his other hand just beside mine in the sheets. Shep turns my head and kisses me properly.

I'm almost angry at how good he is at kissing. I could kiss him all night and be satisfied. I won't tell him that because I really want to come. His knee slips between my thighs and nudges them apart just a little bit, leaving just enough room for his hand. His whole hand is cupping my pussy. I'm so wet I know I'm soaking all of his palm. He slides three fingers in and swirls them around just for a moment before he's cupping me again.

"Shep," I beg.

"Shhh. I got you." He licks the side of my mouth. "Just hold tight, baby." His yanks my head to the side. I let out a little yelp, but the pain just spurs me on. I need him inside of me. Shep sits back a little and his other hand is back between my legs, but it's not enough. It's just a tease. And then I feel his knuckles brushing over my ass. Over and over.

"Do you feel that?" he asks. I try to nod, but he's still gripping my hair.

"Yes," I say.

"I'm using everything I got from that dripping wet cunt of yours to jack my dick."

My body reacts on its own. I wince because I'm so turned on at the thought of it, I try to move, but I can't. He's holding my hair too tight.

"You want me to fuck you, don't you?"

"Yes," I say. "Please," I beg.

"Soon," he whispers and then he's kissing me again.

This torture continues. I can feel his hand and his cock on my ass and at the base of my back and every few minutes he pauses to gather more of my juices from between my legs. His kisses become more frantic, more restless. He starts getting rough. I bite him, but not too hard. He bites me back, just hard enough. Then I know what's about to happen.

"I'm about to come," he says. His voice sounds so ragged. I close my eyes. "Fuck," he says and then he says it again a little louder and then I feel it on my ass. The hot drops covering my skin, then the head of his cock spreading it around. He releases my hair and lets out several deep breath before he speaks again.

"I just came all over your ass. You want to see?"

"Yes," I gasp. I turn my head and watch him as he grabs his phone. I lie there as he snaps a few pictures.

"You wanna taste it?" he asks.

"Yes," I say even louder. I feel his fingers wiping up what they can. He covers me again with his whole body and holds the phone up in front of my face so I can see how nice my ass looks all red and painted.

"Open up." I do and he shoves two cum covered fingers in my mouth. I swirl my tongue around, then suck them clean. He's salty and sweet. "Next, I do it on your tits and then in your mouth. Don't move."

"'Kay,"I say as he hops up. I lay there and hold still as I hear the sink running in the other room. He's back a few seconds later and I feel the warmth of a wet wash cloth smoothing over my butt. Then he gives it a hard slap, and I hear the wet sound of the washcloth landing in his hamper. He leaves the room again. He's shutting off the lights in the kitchen. He turns off the lights in the bedroom when he comes back, then moves me to the side of the bed so he can shift the covers out from under me.

"It's time for bed," he says as he pulls me into his arms.

"Now?"

"Yes."

"Can we finish?" I turn my head and look at him. His eyes are closed.

"We are finished."

"I didn't come yet."

"So? You wanted me to come on you. I did. It's time for bed."

"What?" I roll all the way over.

"You can come when you stop talking back to me."

"Um, excuse me sir, but I have hands that work very well."

"I'm sure they do, but I don't sleep that deep. You try finishing yourself off before morning." He rolls me back over and spoons me. I stare into the darkness and think about all the ways out of this. My mind is still turning over, but my body eventually gives up. I hate this game, but I can't stop myself from wanting to play it so badly. I let out a rageful sigh and sag against him. I've never been more annoyed with a spent cock pressing against my ass in my whole life.

"Atta girl," he says. I almost reconsider the blaze and the K9 theft.

CHAPTER FOURTEEN

SHEP

I can't remember the last time I've woken up feeling so smug, but I get some extreme pleasure from sending Claudia to bed wet and unsatisfied. I am not sure whether or not she's broken the only rule I've set for her, but the few times I wake during the night and she's peacefully sleeping in my arms or curled up against my side, her hands are nowhere near her crotch.

I'm still pissed at Jad for the shit he pulled over dinner, but Claudia is a nice distraction and I try not to think of that in all the ways it could be shitty. Her presence calms me and for the time being it's nice to remember there are other people who don't live on the mountain. I don't mind the sex all that much either.

My alarm goes off at its usual time. I sit up, then roll to the other side of the bed and wake her up. She jerks a little, but doesn't try to punch or elbow me. Definitely an improvement.

"Baby, wake up."

"Hey," she says, still groggy. "I'm up. What are we doing?"

"Every morning I go out and photograph different parts of the mountain. You're coming with me."

"Okay."

She shuffles to the edge of the mattress and stands. I watch her as she gets her bearings and starts digging through her things.

I sit on the edge of the other side of the bed and don't realize I'm staring at her until she turns and looks at me.

"What?"

"I'm not gonna lie. I was starting to like the way you always argue with me. I didn't expect you to come along so willingly."

Maybe she's finally settled into the time difference and she's too tired to argue. It is well before dawn. She goes into the bathroom and when she comes back I can smell the mint of her toothpaste coming off of her. I pull on my socks and watch her as she puts lotion on her face.

"Push back turning you on?" she says as she slips on her bra.

"A little bit."

"I mean, I can make today a living hell for you, you just say the word, Master Shep."

I pull on my shirt and walk over to her as she's hopping into her jeans.

"I'll think about it. Coffee sound good?"

"Yes please."

I finish getting ready. We have our coffee and we head out. We head west again and I lead Claudia down the trail. She doesn't say much, but I do laugh when she jumps at the sound of a screech owl. She slaps my arm and laughs quietly when she realizes she's not in mortal danger. She finally speaks up though when we hit the clearing.

"This is where we came the other day."

"Yeah." I hand her Titus's leash and set my gear down on the rock ledge. There's still another fifteen or so minutes before sunrise. "I'm doing a series for the forest service and the Smithsonian called New Day. I've been photographing sunrises for almost five years."

"Jesus. Is there an end point?"

"I'm aiming for a twenty-year series. When I was a kid I did a project for school on global warming and my grandfather was telling me how you could see subtle difference in the climate. You know, he'd noticed that the winters were shorter, summers hotter since he moved into the cabin, but it was the last ten or fifteen years they started really noticing differences in the migration patterns of some of the birds and the butterflies. The water levels of the streams and rivers, even the foliage. I wanted to visually document changes in the mountain as a whole. Some universities have been using some of my stuff too."

"That's really cool. And a little bit frightening. We're all gonna die."

"Too true. But this will all go on, unless we nuke the planet down the center. I'll show you more of my shots from this spot when we get back."

I look out over the Western rise and start snapping photos of that side of the valley. Claudia is quiet beside me, only whispering to Titus every now and then when he tries to convince her to follow him on an adventure into the trees. The sun crests over the peak in the East and I am able to capture the perfect outline of its shadow. When I have what I want, I lean on the bolder next to Claudia.

"You in a hurry to head back? Are you hungry?"

"A little. But we don't need to rush. It's nice up here."

I lift my camera off my chest and turn to her. "Do you mind?"

Her eyes go a little wide for a moment, but then she shakes her head. "Do I need to pose or act natural?"

"Do what feels right."

"'Kay," she says. Then she crosses her eyes and sticks out her tongue at me. Then she's smiling and then she's making a kissy face. "Wait, get me with my new best buddy." She hops off the boulder and squats next to Titus and I get a few shots of him trying to lick her face and Claudia laughing.

"Okay it's my turn." I watch her as she takes her phone out of her coat pocket and turns its camera on me. "You ready?"

I try not to roll my eyes. "Yeah, sure." I never intentionally smile in pictures.

"Let me help you." She steps in front of me and starts snapping selfies of us both. I cave and kiss her forehead and she's able to capture that. Then she turns to me. "I fucking hate when people do this, but whatever." She leans up and kisses me and when she pulls back, she pulls up her photo album. She'd managed to snap two slightly crooked pictures of us kissing.

"See the light here? I wanted this to express the elements of hopefulness and helplessness that plague the modern, yet slightly older millennials," she says.

"We should frame it."

"You want me to send it to you? As soon as we get back to your place 'cause there is no service out here." She sings the last bit.

"Yeah, send me all of them. And I'll email you the photos I took."

"Thank you." She leans against my arm and I shift my camera out of the way and wrap my arm around her shoulder. I want to tell her that I'm enjoying the mountain in a different way now that she's here. I want to tell her that she's making the trek out to these more remote spots easier. She's quieting the dull buzz in my head that usually comes with the noises of the forest. I like having her with me.

"What brought your grandfather up here?" she asks.

"The tent boom in the seventies."

"What?" She looks up at me. She has this little smile on her face.

"Lightweight tent engineering was a game changer. They needed more rangers and he was the first to show up."

"And now here you are."

"Yup." A natural silence falls between us again. I just need to enjoy this morning and not think ahead. She's going to leave, she has to. I pull her closer and kiss the top of her head. And then I hear it. Movement on the trail.

"There's some people coming, that way," I say as I nod to where the trail splits down to the southwest It's less worn, more overgrown and not the way I usually travel to this point.

She stands away from me and I watch her as she presses her hands behind her against the boulder. She swallows and keeps her eyes trained on the trees.

"You okay?" I ask.

"Yeah. I'm fine," she says, but her eyes have suddenly gone wild.

A few moments later two hikers come up the trail, two women. One Black, one Asian. They're holding hands even though they're loaded down with gear.

"Good morning," the Black woman says in a chipper voice.

"Morning," I reply with a nod.

"Glad to see we're not the only ones up to witness God's glory at this ungodly hour."

"It's the best time to witness it," I say.

"Beautiful dog," the other woman says. She holds her hand out as they come closer and smiles when Titus gives her palm a lick of hello. "Hey, buddy," she coos.

"You guys local?" the Black woman asks.

"I am, yeah. You heading up to Dixon's Peak?"

"Yes," they both laugh.

"Is there a shortcut? We want to get up there by lunchtime," the Asian woman says.

"This is the best way. The only shortcut I know of involves a helicopter ride over a ravine. You should be at the site by eleven if you keep a steady pace."

"We better keep moving, babe," The Black woman says. She has the look in her eye. I'm sure there's a proposal at the end of their hike.

"Yeah. Thanks for the tip. You have a good one."

"No problem. Enjoy the view."

Both women nod their goodbyes and I watch them for half a second then look back to Claudia. She's not breathing right. I slip my lens cap on then run my hand down her back.

"You okay?"

"Yeah. No. I'm not sure," she says. Her voice is shaky.

I step in front of her and lift her head with my finger under her chin. Her pupils are all fucked up. I step closer and smooth my hands over her shoulders.

"Breathe. In and out."

She closes her eyes and drops her head to my chest. We stay like that for a few minutes until she lets out a deep sigh and straightens up. Her eyes are almost back to normal, but her breathing is still a little shaky. I touch the side of her face and her neck.

"Sorry," she says.

"You don't have to apologize. Are you alright?"

"Yeah. I'm not sure. Maybe it was the sound. It got really loud up here all of a sudden. I wasn't expecting to see other people up here."

"Are you afraid to run into other people up here?" I ask. Anything she says will make sense. I just want to make sure I understand.

"I'm... I can't explain it. I just got—I just freaked out."

"I got what I need so we can head back and we don't have to come back out for the rest of the week if you don't want to."

"No, no." She waves me off but she still lets out another deep breath. "I just wasn't expecting to see people."

"We can head back anyway. You want some breakfast."

"Yeah. Food would be good."

"Come on. You got, Titus?" I ask. That seems to shock her back to her senses.

She looks down at her hand and looks at her grip on Titus's leash. "Yeah. Yes, I got him."

We take our time heading back down the trail. She doesn't say a word the whole time.

*

Food seems to help. She tells me after she eats that she thinks she had a panic attack.

"I'm not ignoring it," she says. "I just—yeah. I'm okay. Really. I just need to figure out what that was all about."

She lets me hold her and kiss her since I have nothing helpful to say. She sits with me while I upload my images. She gives me her email so I can send along the pictures I took of her. I try not to stare at them for too long as I transfer the files. She knows she looks good, but she doesn't know how beautiful she is. She doesn't know what her beauty does to me.

She texts the pictures she took of us to my phone. I glance at them to make sure they came through. I won't look at them again until she's gone. I can't. I have a conference call with our dev team. After, I explain to Claudia more about what I do. She watches TV while I spend the rest of the day working.

At 2:30, Carla from the post office calls to let me know my stuff has arrived. I tell Claudia we'll head into town at four. She nods off after my second meeting and then I wake her up so we can leave. She seems one hundred percent back to herself when she tells me to hold the fuck on until she can brush her teeth.

She's chatty on the ride down, telling me on the way about a group chat she's in with some friends she's known since high school. One of their husbands is cheating and they are trying to decide whether or not he should die slowly and how much of an accident his death should look like. She cusses me and the mountain for the shitty service when I tell her she should get a signal once we get back into town, in another fifteen minutes.

"He could be dead by then!" she yells at me and then she laughs.

"Sorry. You'll just have to miss out on all of those counts of conspiracy."

"You are no fun." When we reach the bottom of the hill, her phone starts vibrating like crazy and I'm getting the full play by play of their plan to deal with Brendan, the asshole, soon-to-be ex and possibly dead husband. She stays in the car while I run into the post office.

"I just don't understand how you cheat like that," she says once I'm back behind the wheel.

"You got me," I say with a shrug. I glance over at her and smile even though her face is glued to her phone. I leave her to it until we pull up to the store. I park and slip my hand around the back of her neck. She's typing frantically. I realize she's only really been in contact with her friend Liz. I wonder if her other friends know she's here.

"You want to come in or you want to tell me your shoe size and I'll surprise you?"

She looks up from her phone and stares at the large sign hanging over the double wooden doors right in front of my truck. The noise she makes is part cackle, part hacking cough. "Doug Wilmer's Sportsman's Gear Emporium?"

"The Wilmer name has been a staple of Quinten County for over seventy years."

"And I'm sure Doug the seventh is working the register right now."

"Close. The fourth."

"Not the same. Let's go get me some boots." We head inside and Doug Wilmer's great-great grandson, Dougie the fifth, is actually working the register. Claudia calls me a liar when she learns the truth. We head to the back and she picks out a pair of boots. Dougie grabs her size and leaves us to try them on.

I know she doesn't need me to, but I squat in front of her and pull her knee-high boot off. She's wearing these white knit socks that make her feet look adorable and dainty. I feel her eyes on me as I take her heel in my hand and help her wiggle her foot into the less sexy hiking boot.

"My prince," she says with a smile.

"How does that feel?"

"I never thought I'd buy another pair of these things again." She turns her head to the side and looks closer at the boot, but I can tell her mind is on her brother.

"I take it you didn't pick up gear here before?"

"No," she shakes her head. "Miles gave me a list of woodsy things and I picked everything up in the city before I came out here. He took care of everything else, like the tents and stuff. Damn that lightweight technology."

"We will not be camping. I promise." I run my hand up her leg and give her calf a little squeeze.

"I know," she leans forward and kisses me. "They fit great."

"You want to wear them out?" I say as I reach over and pick up her other boots.

"I probably should. Break them in a little. Are we getting dinner next?"

"Yep."

"Should I leave my bra here just in case you want easy tit access?"

"A bra isn't likely to stop me." We head up to the register and listen as Dougie tells us at length that Claudia made a great choice in boots.

"If it was warmer you could hike down to Doe's lake, but it's a little too cool to take a dip. Unless you're into that sort of thing."

"No," Claudia says with a little laugh. "Polar bearing is not my idea of a good time."

Dougie nods in my direction, but keeps his eyes on Claudia. "Have him take you up to Dixon's Peak. Great views from up there. And you can be up and back in a day. No need to camp."

I look at Dougie as he glances between us and I realize that he at least has an idea of who Claudia is. I'm tempted to skip dinner and take her back up to the house.

"Well thanks, Dougie. We're gonna head to the Notch tomorrow actually."

"Oh another great spot. Enjoy."

I take Claudia's hand and walk her out to the car. "Everyone knows, don't they? They know I'm the girl who almost got murdered and now I'm back."

"You've been here a few days and people do talk. Especially Jad and May-Bell. And no one has seen me with a women in three years."

"I guess that's to be expected in such a small town."

"Doesn't hurt that you're so beautiful either," I say to distract her even though it's the truth.

"Ugly girl would breeze right through this place, huh? No questions asked?"

"Pretty much."

"Like I said, such a prince."

I wink at her and nudge her toward the passenger door with a hand on her butt. We head over to Connie's. It seems pretty quiet, but I almost slam my truck into reverse and floor it back to my house when I see Sarah's Tahoe in the parking lot. I pull in between it and Connie's truck. I take a deep breath. I've seen Sarah more times than I'd appreciate since she moved back to town. I can stomach it. I can, but Jad opened up some old wounds and I can't pretend that everything between Sarah and I is completely okay. I know I will be, but I don't want to act civil.

"That's Sarah's car," I say.

"Oh. Do you want to go somewhere else?"

"The nearest place with real food this time of day is forty minutes away and I really want to crack that box open."

She glances over her shoulder at the massive box of kink related devices and apparel. "Let's go in."

"You're sure?"

"Yeah. I got this. Plus, we don't have to sit with her."

"True."

She flashes me a big grin and hops out of the truck. I'm right behind her and wait for her to come around to the other side so I can take her hand. Just as we cross the short distance of the gravel lot, the door to Connie's swings open and out comes Sarah with a takeout bag in her hand. She takes half a step and then almost trips down the stairs. Claudia and I both stop walking at the same time.

Sarah quickly recovers though and lets out a manic laugh. She waves. "Hi. Hey!"

"Sarah," I say.

"Hi." She comes down the stairs with more success this time. She glances at our hands. "Claudia, I didn't know you were still in town." I know she's lying. Her voice gets really high when she lies. "What are you two—what are you two up to?"

"Uh we just came down to run some errands and grab something to eat," Claudia says.

"Cool, cool! How long are you in town? Thank you again for the flowers. They're on my dining room table." Another lie. She lives with her sister and they don't have a dining room table. My best guess is that she threw them out the second someone in town told her about us.

"Oh, good," Claudia says. "It's an open-ended trip right now." She looks up at me and smiles. "Didn't seem right to fly cross-country, drive all the way into town just to see this guy for like five minutes, so I'm hanging out for a little while. I finally got another pair of proper boots so we can explore a little." She lifts up her foot and I think Sarah is going to throw up or her eyes are going to explode.

"Oh wow! Cute. You're going hiking?" she says, nervously.

"Just a little in the morning. I know. You'd think the woods up there would be literally the last place I'd want to be, but Shep here knows what he's doing and he's proven I can trust his aim with a shotgun." Claudia's voice gets really tight at the end. Sarah blinks and almost takes a fraction of a step back.

"Too true," she says. "He is pretty protective."

I've had enough at this point. I gently squeeze Claudia's hand. "You ready to eat?"

"Yeah," she says. "Thank you again." She lets go of my hand and hugs Sarah. I'm not sure what to think. Neither does Sarah, from the look on her face.

"Oh! You're welcome. Just doing a nurse's duty." She pulls back and gives me a tight smile. I keep my expression blank. "Enjoy your supper."

"Thanks," we both say at the same time in a way that I know unsettles Sarah even more. I can't drag this shit out a second longer. I lead Claudia inside.

I'm sure Connie knows all about what happened between me and Jad, but she greets us with her usual smile and gives us the booth in the back. The few people in there don't pay too much attention to us.

"That was interesting," I say once we're sitting down.

"Whatever. She's not my fucking therapist and she fucked with you. She's not gonna comment in any kind of way on how either of us are coping or how we spend our time."

"Is this you pissed off?"

"No, just mildly irritated. Why, does me being pissed turn you on?"

I shake my head. It's doesn't. "No. You sticking up for yourself was hot, but not the idea of you being worked into a frenzy or the idea of something upsetting you. Just wondering."

"No, I know it's not my business per se, but I don't like what she did to you. You might only be mine for a limited time, but you're still mine. You don't fuck with what's mine," she says with a little shake of her head.

"You need a moment with the menu?" I ask.

"Yeah give me a sec." She flips it over then unzips her jacket. Then pulls up her shirt and pulls her tits out of her bra. "Okay let's see. How's the BLT?"

I know she's leaving at the end of the week, but in that moment I want to marry Claudia Deja Cade.

CHAPTER FIFTEEN

I tell Claudia to put her tits away so I can enjoy my meal without distraction. She gives me lip for ruining her fun. I ignore her and go back to my food. My cock is hard under the table the whole meal and I'm not in the mood to even fuck with foreplay until we get back to my house. Once I get started I have no intention of stopping. We finish our food and Connie sends us back up the mountain with a fresh apple ginger pie. She doesn't say anything, but I'm sure it's partially a peace offering from May-Bell.

Claudia accepts it with a smile and a thank you. I thank Connie as well, but she knows I know. I can tell by the bashful grin on her face. We head back up to my place and I'm a little shocked that Claudia is so quiet. I don't complain though.

I also try not to notice how strange it feels when she offers to open the gate to my property and hops out before I can stop her, or how comfortable and normal it feels when she grabs the pie and my keys and opens the front door for me while I carry the big box inside. She asks if we should take Titus out before we get started. I kiss her before I say yes. We take care of Titus and then it's time for us.

I put my gear away in the office and then heft the box up on the dining room table. I pull out my knife and hold it out toward her.

"You want to do the honors?" I ask.

"Nah, you do it."

I shrug, then flip the blade open and slice open the taped seal.

"Should I record this and we can post a haul video?"

"What?"

"Nothing. Show me what's in your big box." I pull everything out item by item and Claudia takes her turn picking up and handling everything. She picks up one of the large dildos still in its plastic packaging.

"You want to sit on that now while we get ready?" I ask.

"Sure. Let me just bend over and you can shove it right in. I won't even take off my pants."

"You think that won't work but I'm stronger than I look and those pants look pretty thin."

"Ha! No. We're not using all of this tonight are we?"

"Yes. All of it. It's all going in your various orifices. Even the box."

"Shit, I really should stretch."

"Here's what we're going to use tonight." I set aside the rope, the lube, the body oil, one of the floggers, the ball gag, the wrist and ankle cuffs. I consider the blindfold, but skip over it. We'll use that tomorrow. "How do you feel about this?"

She considers the new pile for a moment. She grabs the box of condoms and adds it. "I really need you to fuck me tonight."

"I need to fuck you tonight, so good call there. Anything else you want to add?"

She stares at the table for a long time before she turns to me. She bothers her bottom lip with her finger nails. Then she reaches for one of the three butt plugs and adds it to the pile. It's the metal plug with a blue jewel at the base.

"You ever used one of those before?" I ask.

"Can't say that I have, Master Shep." She's being sarcastic, but I can hear the nerves in her tone. A small bit of pride swells in my chest and something else, maybe a bit of possessiveness. I like that she's taking this seriously. I pick up that plug and switch it out with a small silicone one.

"I've been told that the metal ones aren't as comfortable for long wear or if you're moving around a lot."

"Oh, why'd you get it then?"

I shrug. "Thought we both might like the look of it when it's shoved up your ass."

"We'll save that one for a more glamorous photoshoot later on this week."

"Deal." I turn to her and run my hand over her shoulders. "Do you have any more questions?"

She lets out a deep breath. "No. I think I'm good."

"Okay. Go hop in the shower and I'm going to get everything set up. When you're done, call for me. I'm going to dry you off and help you with your lotion."

She swallows before she answers. "Okay."

"Go on." I watch her until she closes the bathroom door behind her. I look over at Titus who is watching the bathroom door from his bed. "You like her too don't you, buddy." He glances at me and then focuses his attention back on the door. We're both pretty hopeless at this point.

I box up everything we're not using and stash it back in the office first and then I rig up the ropes. I take my time securing them over the exposed beams. I test the ring hook on the far wall. I haven't used it in years, but it's still soundly embedded in the wood.

Then I tear the butt plug from its secure plastic wrapping and wash it with hot water and soap. I unscrew the caps from the lube and the lotion and throw away the safety seals. I grab the remotes and turn on the stereo and then find my favorite artists playlist of ambient music. I adjust the volume and then I wait.

I remind myself to focus. Claudia isn't Sarah. She isn't Meegan. She's none of the women I've been with since I started to discover who I really am. She's unique to me and to this experience and I have to make it great for her. I go over to the sink and get us each a glass of water and set those on the table. I grab a few spare dish rags just in case.

I wait some more.

I take a few deep breaths. I stretch. I pick up the flogger and run the leather between my fingers. It's been a while, but my hands and my wrists know the way. I snap it through the air and my nerve endings instantly react to the sound. We're going to have a good time.

I set it back on the table and pace some more. I'm not in a rush, but I can't help but watch the clock. Ten minutes later the door cracks open. Claudia sticks her head out.

"Shep," she says. Her voice is low, but I can hear her just fine.

I cross the room and join her in the bathroom, which is hot and damp from the steam of her shower. She backs up toward the sink with her hands clasped by her shoulder. Her arms are covering her tits. I grab a towel from the linen shelves and turn toward her. I start with her face and then move to her hair. I know it'll be a while before it's completely dry, but I wring out her thick black hair anyway. "Once we're done in here, let's put your hair up. Keep it out of the way."

"Okay," she squeaks out. I move down to her shoulders and then her back, wiping the droplets of water that are trickling their way down her amazing skin. Before I can stop myself, I bend over and catch a few drops running down her side with my tongue. She jerks in surprise, but holds still when my gaze meets hers. I do it again on her left side and this time I bite her a little. She sighs. I squat on the floor and move to her legs.

"There's not going to be much more talking between now and when we finish. I want you to focus on your body and what sensations you're feeling, and less on a how witty you can be. Are you okay with that?"

I look up and she just nods.

"If I'm right, you are thinking a lot about what's going to happen tonight and you're a little in your head about it. Am I right?"

"Yeah," she says, but her voice is really rough. She clears her throat, but doesn't offer anything else.

"It's called the sub space." I lift up her foot and put it on my knee. I slowly dry off every inch. Even her toes are cute. I switch to the other foot. "We don't need to talk about it at length right now, but it's normal. You're focusing on a lot of emotions and it's going to make you feel a certain way. Just go with it and if you want to talk about it later, we definitely will."

"Okay," she says.

I dry between her thighs and wipe down her ass before I stand. "Where's your lotion?" She turns and grabs the pump bottle of white cream off the counter. I want to take my time, but there's a second part to this rub down and I would like to get her tied up properly before I start. I lotion her whole body, she helps me with her face. I watch her, the way her thick eyelashes almost touch her cheeks as she rubs her face. There are tears slicking her eyelids.

I gently sweep the moisture away with my thumb. I lean down and kiss her on the mouth. She kisses me back, just a firm press with her lips, but I think that's all she can manage at the moment. She's in that headspace for sure. There's no need to try and take her out of it and either way I don't think it would work. You can't talk someone out of a deep emotional space.

I let her know we're good to go and she reminds me she still needs to grab a hair tie out of the bedroom. We make our pitstop there and then I take her hand and lead her out to the great room and over to the dining table.

"Bend over," I tell her. She leans over the table and I admire her pretty round ass as I grab the silicone butt plug and slick it up with lube. "Relax for me." I watch carefully as I press the curved end into her tightest hole. She takes it like a pro, pushing back to give the proper room for me to slide it in. She exhales when it's seated to the base, then stands and turns to face me even though I didn't tell her to. I decide to let it slide.

"I'm going to gag you. Let me know if you don't want me to."

"No, it's fine," she says quietly. "I want to try it."

"Good. Don't try to swallow. You're going to drool. Just let it happen." She opens her mouth and holds still as I slip the rubber ball inside her lips. I secure the small buckle behind her head and then look her over to make sure it's not biting into her skin.

"Good? Nod for me." She nods and gives me a thumbs up. "Instead of hedgehog, if you want to stop just snap your fingers. If you forget to snap just shout 'Stop'. I'll be able to hear you." She nods again, gives me another thumbs up. I go for the leather cuffs next and she lets me move her arms and feet where I need them so I can secure them around her wrists and ankles. She doesn't say a word as I tie the rope around the metal attachment points of the cuffs.

"I'm going to hoist your hands above your head, but not so high that your feet won't be comfortable on the floor. Nod if that's okay." She nods. I start pulling. When her arms are perfectly stretched above her head, I attach the rope to the mounted ring then walk back over to her side. "That good?" She nods and lets out a muffled "Yes."

"Good. We're going to begin now." I step back and finally take a good look at her whole body. There's something about having a woman spread out for you, something about the sight of every inch of her on display. I pick up the flogger and step closer to Claudia. She glances at the leather tails for a second, then focuses back on my face.

I step behind her and get more of this perfect view. I move closer, press my hard on against the small of her back. I hear the rush of air that comes out of her nose. I wrap both my arms around her waist and and twist my wrist just enough so the flogger sweeps back and forth across her stomach and her thighs.

"I'm going to use this on you tonight," I say in her ear. "I'm going to use it mostly on your back and a little on your ass. Your tits are going to be spared. How does that sound to you?

She lets out a muffled "Good. Great."

I reach down and tilt her head to the side. I take my sweet time running my tongue over the curve of her neck. She lets out this long, pitiful moan so I do it again. I bite and lick and suck at her, grinding my dick against her back until I can't stand it anymore. I kiss her skin and release her. I walk back around to the front of her body.

She's doing her best to hold still, but I can see the little tremors rippling all over her body. I step close again and tell her to look at me. Drool is already running down her chin. I want to hate how badly it turns me on. It's only been a few minutes and she's already giving in. She's already losing control. There's only one more thing I need.

"Do you like this?"

She nods.

"I thought so. You look like you like it a lot. I like it too. It feels like you're finally mine. Do you have any idea how good it feels to know that you're mine? Even for just one night or one week. You're mine. Do you want to be mine?"

She nods frantically and lets out another muffled "Yes."

"That's exactly what I want to hear." I lean down and kiss both her cheeks. "This isn't about pain. We're just gonna get you nice and warm. Nice and loose. Just relax and let me take care of you." There's no response, she just searches my eyes. I keep the words that are bouncing around in my head to myself. It's time.

I move behind her and take a few deep breaths and then I swing. The tails connect with the smooth skin of her upper back. She jerks a bit and makes a little noise. I wait a beat and strike her again, on the other side of her upper back. Another jerk and a moan, but she settles just as quickly. I strike again, a little lower and again on the other side. I work in a circular motion, again picking up speed but barely increasing intensity. I watch closely, listen carefully for every sound she makes. The little moans and squeaks. All of it rolls over my own skin. All of it permeates my senses. She's perfect.

I stop momentarily and walk around to check on her. There are tears running down her face. I don't ask her any questions. I don't want to make her think. I just wipe her cheeks with my thumbs and kiss her skin.

"You're doing very well, baby. I'm very pleased." She squeezes her eyes shut and more tears leak out. I kiss her again and step back around her body. I smooth my hand over her upper back. Her skin is warm, but nowhere near welting. We can go a while longer. I step back and roll my shoulder. I stretch my neck again. I've been lying to myself about how badly I need this. I haven't been honest with myself when it comes to how often I need this. This is months in the making, maybe years.

We've only been at it no more than ten minutes and I know it's never been this way before. Never with Meegan or any of the others before her. It's never been this way with Sarah. That's for fuck sure. It's her. I know it. It's Claudia. Everything about her and everything she's given me up to this moment. Her smartass mouth and how quick she is to turn that shit on its head to offer me her enthusiastic submission. I believe her when she tells me she wants this. Even if it's just tonight, she is mine. I need to be inside her soon.

Another deep breath and my flogger connects with her ass. The stroke is harder than the ones that kissed her back. I almost groan at the way her ass cheek bounces. A flash of red colors that gorgeous brown skin. I give the other side of her ass the same treatment. Another flash of red and then another. She yelps louder this time. I know the sting is more intense, but she is handling it so well. I swing again and again. I set a rhythm, a pace, and soon she starts to wiggle her ass in toward my flogger, trying to anticipate each blow. She's begging for it. I find that sweet spot where my arm is perfectly warm and the sweat is starting to build on my own back.

I feel that control I've been looking for, the momentum. No need to swing any harder—just faster, in perfect time with the pounding of my heart. I do move faster and she can't follow the swings. Too fast for her to move any direction to chase whatever sensation she thinks I'm denying her. We both know that's a lie. I'm giving her everything. I'm giving it all to her and there's more. She knows. It's just her mind can't keep up. Fighting what's already happening to her body. Those endorphins are hitting their tipping point and any moment now she's going to come.

And then it starts to happen. Her legs start to shake. I don't stop. She lets out one long, consistent moan. I step behind her and wrap my arm around her body. I shove my fingers between her legs. Her head jerks to the side as she cries out. She so wet, so fucking wet and her clit is swollen hard, just begging. I ignore it and shove three fingers inside her tight cunt. It's so fucking slick, I slide right in. I'm not gentle. I shake my fingers hard and that long moan pitches even higher. She almost head butts me in the chin as she shoots up to her tiptoes.

"Come, baby. Come for me," I say. "Come all over my fucking hand. Squeeze me." I feel her bearing down. I keep shaking my fingers and I know I'm hitting that spot. She fills my palm, soaks my wrists and soon it's running down the inside of her thighs. She's practically screaming but I won't stop until I'm ready. She keeps shaking. Her chest is moving up and down. I swear I can hear her heart beating or the sound of my heartbeat is filling up the whole room. She soaks my hand two more times before I withdraw and slowly step away. I wipe her wetness on her thigh. Then reach for the lube and a condom.

I watch her as I get myself ready. I've worked her out pretty good. Her head is slumping on her shoulders and her wrists are carrying all her weight. Her knees are done. She keeps squeezing her eyes shut. She blacked out momentarily, but I think she can take a little more. I move back behind her and gently spread her cheeks. They are still glowing hot. It's hard not to stand there and just admire my handiwork while I ease the plug out of her. She whimpers again and shivers as I slip it out.

"Shhh," I tell her. "You won't be empty for long."

I set the plug on the table and slick my cock with some more lube before I gently start to press my way in. Claudia takes me beautifully. I hear her breathing instantly change and I can feel the way she's relaxing and flexing her muscles to let every inch of me up that perfect ass of hers. I know I'm not gonna last long. She's so fucking tight and hot and the smell of her pussy is all around me still coating my hand and forearm. I need to come.

I grip her hips gently then lick the shell of her ear before I ease out and push back in. I slip my hand around and finger her sweet clit again. I pinch it hard and she shoots back up to her tiptoes, making this noise that I know will be a part of my jerk off fantasies for the rest of my life. My left hand is still on her hip and I use it to give me the leverage I need to pound in and out of her. I keep squeezing that clit of hers until she comes and this time I'm with her. That pressure shoots up my balls, all the way to the crown of my head and I think about just how amazing it would be to fill her with my cum one day.

I think I black out for a second and when I come back myself, we're both still shaking a bit. I need more time, but she needs me now. I can't leave her restrained anymore. I gently ease out of her and discard the condom in the trash, then zip up my pants.

When I come back to her she's definitely something to look at. Drool lining her body from her bottom lip past her navel. Her thighs still dripping wet and there's a small puddle at her toes. I undo the ball gag and immediately she sighs and grinds her back teeth. I grab a towel and quickly wipe down her thighs and drop the towel on the floor, then I remove her hands from the cuffs. I catch her as she falls into my arms and swoop her up. I use my foot to cover the wet spot she's left behind on the floor, before I move her to the couch.

"Better?" I ask. She nods and then I feel it. Her whole body draws up, every inch of her chest and then the sound comes out. She doesn't cry, she weeps, sobs against my chest. I cradle her head, kiss her face, rub every inch of her back. It's a while before she stops, but I expected it to be this intense. We've both been keeping a lot in.

Eventually she rolls her head against my chest and rubs her cheek against my shirt. I laugh a little but I don't care that she's using my Henley as a tissue.

"Better?"

"I don't even know. That was crazy."

"Crazy bad or crazy good?"

"Good. Surreal. I think I'm still having an out of body experience."

"You were fucking amazing," I say. "I'll give you some water in a minute and then I'm gonna use that massage oil on every inch of your beautiful, sore, used up body and then I'm going to put you to bed."

"I want you to come to bed with me."

"I will, baby," I say. "I'm not going anywhere."

CHAPTER SIXTEEN

CLAUDIA

Shep said I would feel a little weird, something about a sub space, but I feel more than weird once we're finished. I can't even begin to describe how good it is. I don't even know if I'll tell Liz about it. Her staunch commitment to the bachelorette life has led to her having a more varied and exciting sex life than mine, but I don't know if I'll be able to vocalize what happens between Shep and I. He follows through on his promise. We stay on the couch for a while. He gives me all the water I could handle, two full glasses that he tells me to sip slowly. I chug the second glass. Then he takes me to the bedroom and he brings the massage oil with us. He didn't joke when he said he was going to rub down every inch of my body.

He lays on the bed and takes his time massaging my shoulders, all the way down to my hands. He massages my fingers and explains that I'd be surprised how random parts of the body can be inexplicably sore after sessions as intense as the one we'd just experienced. My brain tries to come up with words to respond. Something about how he did lie or how I wasn't expecting any of this to really happen, but I can't because my brain isn't working right. So I just nod. Or I just agree with him in my head.

After he finishes with my feet, he tells me he was going to shut down the house and get in bed with me. He asks if I need anything else. I ask about that pie. He comes back with it and his laptop. I pick at the crust as I watch him strip naked and try not to climb all the way into his lap while we watch more of my Netflix choices. Shep is sweet and attentive. He only tells me once that my choices in entertainment are terrible and I know he's half joking. When I ask him to kiss me, he does. I still don't feel right though. I cannot put my finger on it, but something is wrong.

I feel a little better when Shep wakes me up in the morning. It's early again. The sun isn't up. Shep has me sit up when he turns on the light and he looks me over. He's checking for bruising he says, but he doesn't find any. He asks me how I feel. I tell him I'm okay, but I feel a little strange and I feel a little strange about him, like I won't exactly feel right if he's not holding me. I know I've said that before, but this time it feels a little different.

He tells me I'm experiencing something called sub drop. I'll be feeling a little wonky, maybe fore the rest of the day, but he won't leave me. He'll hold me as much as I want. He pulls me into his arms. He kisses my face. I almost tell him that I think we should stay in bed, but I keep that to myself and we shower together and then we get dressed.

He hands me Titus's leash and we head out into the darkness. We go a different way this time. The trail is narrower and Shep has me walk in front of him. "Titus knows the way," he says. I don't say anything, I just hold on and let this massive beast of a dog drag me through the wilderness. It's colder than before. I know this kind of cold even though there's something different to it in the city.

It's going to snow at some point. I regret not bringing my hat, but I don't want to pull up my hood even though my ears are getting cold. I want to be able to hear everything. It's still dark when we come to this small clearing. There's a break in the trees above though and that lack of coverage makes it light enough to see the tall ferns that grow uninterrupted.

"This is the spot," Shep says. His voice sounds distant to me and I feel like I'm moving in slow motion when I turn to him as he starts to pull his camera out of its bag. Something flashes through me. It's anger maybe. I don't know, it's something, and it's making my skin itchy.

"Kiss me," I say to him.

In the near darkness we're close enough for me to see the corner of his lip turn up under his mustache. He says something, but I don't hear him. I'm not paying attention. And he's moving closer to me anyway so I know it doesn't matter. He kisses me deep and slow. I try to live in that kiss, the way his lips are so smooth and the way his beard feels against my face. I look for what's making me feel so weird in the way his tongue slowly slides against mine. My clit starts to throb and I know if I finger myself I'll be wet in that way that demands a certain kind of attention. My chest hurts when he pulls away and licks his lips.

"When I'm done. Right up against that tree. How does that sound?"

"Good," I say. He smiles again. I know he's happy that he finally has me wrapped around his giant little finger. Whatever a Dominant is supposed to be, he is that. He's great at it. I am subdued. I have submitted. I'll do it again and again. I'll do it up against that tree when he's done documenting the morning sky and the way we're slowly killing our planet. I'll do my best not to let whatever is eating at me choke me before he's ready to show me how manly he can be out in the great wide open.

The sky starts to lighten but there's no sun. I was right, there's cloud cover and the temperature doesn't rise. It'll snow for sure. I search for that electric feeling in the air. It's there and it's makes me even more itchy the moment I realize it. Shep seems focused on the sky and the tops of the trees so I take Titus on a little walk across the clearing. I realize my mistake when I turn around. The clearing is bigger than it looks and Shep is really far away. I go back. He smiles as I come closer.

"Got a great shot of you and the beast here." He holds out the body of his camera and shows me the little digital monitor. I blink a few times and look at the dot of a woman on the monitor.

"You should take nudes of me," I hear myself say.

"You want me to?" he asks.

"Don't you want to?"

"Yes. But later and indoors. It's cold out here."

"But not cold enough to stop you from fucking me up against that tree over there is it?"

"You want me to fuck you?" My pussy throbs at the words. He needs to stop looking at me like that or I might hurt him.

"If you're done, yeah."

"I'm done."

He tucks his camera away and takes Titus's leash from my hand, then leads us both over to the end of the clearing. He loops Titus's leash around a skinny tree then turns on me. I watch the predatory look in his eyes as he carefully pulls his shotgun over his shoulder and sets it on the ground. His camera bag follows and then he's unzipping his jeans and pulling out his erection. I want to suck him, but I keep glancing at the gun. I'm waiting for it to go off. I can hear the sound of it, that ear splitting bang. I can hear it.

Shep's in front of me all of a sudden. I glance down at my new best friend and see he's already slipped a condom on. He's rough when he grips my breast through my jacket. Air rushes out of my mouth.

"I want it," I say. I didn't know I could sound so needy and pathetic but here we are. He unbuttons my jeans and almost snaps my fly with how hard he pulls it down. He spins me around and I steady myself with both my gloved hands on the nearest tree.

He's inside me. I squeeze my eyes shut and bite back a moan. When I open my eyes I look over and see the gun resting on the ground. I can't look away from it. It shouldn't be on the ground. Shep's hand slips around my neck, firm but gentle and he tilts my head up. He's going to kiss me, but I can't take my eyes off the gun. I can feel the air gathering in my lungs but it won't come out. More and more goes in, but it's not coming out. I can't breathe. I shake my head. "Shep. Shep. Wait." He lets me go and I turn around and pull up my pants before he can stop me.

"You okay?"

"No. I can't—I can't do this out here."

"Okay, okay. That's okay. We don't have to." He pulls off the condom and stuffs himself back in his pants.

"Pick up the gun."

He stops moving and fixes me with the weirdest look, like I'm crazy. Like I asked him to shoot me.

"Pick it up."

"Okay." He looks away from me long enough to safely retrieve it from the ground, but his eyes are back on my face the moment he slings it back over his body. "Better?"

"Yes. Thank you. Is sex outdoors a part of your thing?"

"No. I just really wanted you and there was no one around."

"You don't know that," I say before I realize what I'm saying. He looks at me, trying to sort it out.

"We're off any of the public trails. No one comes up here."

"I don't want to do it, okay."

"We don't have to. I would never make you. I just— we're alone up here."

"Can we go back? You're done taking pictures right?"

"Yeah. Yeah, I said I was." He head cocks a bit to the side and I realize I'm scaring him. I scrub my hands over my face and instantly regret closing my eyes. I drop my hands and stare back at him.

"Can we go please? I want to be inside."

"Sure. Let's go." He picks up his camera and I take it from him so he can grab Titus's leash. I don't know what the fuck I'm doing until I'm halfway down the trail. Shep is right behind me and every few feet Titus bumps into my side. He thinks this is a game. That's fine. We can race back to the house. I start running. Shep calls my name but I don't stop. It's light enough. I can see. I can see fine. I know where I'm going and these new boots are easy to run in too. My feet hurt like hell, but it's easy. I just keep my eyes on the break in the trees in front of me. I know exactly where I'm going.

I'm sweating by the time I reach Shep's property. It feels good to run, I realize. I stomp to a stop, my arms flailing, my feet hitting the ground like I've just crossed the finish line on a track.

"Hey!" he says behind me, but I ignore him 'cause my phone is going crazy.

"Hold on. One sec." I pull it out of my pocket. He really should lock his wifi. You get full bars in his yard. There's a bunch of texts from Liz and some voicemails.

Idk if you're up, but call me!

IS THERE SERVICE UP THERE?

I hit the phone icon next to her name and she picks up after the second ring. "Oh thank god!"

"Is everything okay?" I look up at Shep and he's frowning at me, but he doesn't push. He nods toward the house and I follow him and Titus up the front steps.

"Oh my god, sorry. Everything's fine. You will never guess who I ran into."

"Who?"

"Vivianne Coolidge."

"From Mode?" She'd been stuck at a table with Liz and I at a gala two New Year's Eves ago. She hated me, but she and Liz had become instant friends.

"Girl, yes! She asked about you. She didn't know you'd left Kleinman's."

"What did she want?"

"You! She wants you to come to work for her at Mode."

"Shut the fuck up." I know I need to go back to work in a few months, but I haven't started looking and I hadn't even considered sending my resume to Mode.

"I gave her your number and she said she was going to call you as soon as she gets to her office. She wants to talk to you like—" My phone beeps and I look at the screen. It's a 212 area code.

"Shit that could be her."

"Go!"

I don't even say bye before I click over and let out an oddly confident hello. This woman could make or break my career.

"Claudia, love. It's Vivianne Coolidge. I just ran into Elizabeth." I sink down on Shep's couch and listen as she basically tells me she's delighted that I'm not dead and no longer working for Kleinman's and how they want my impeccable taste for their editorial department. She throws out a number that would get me out of my tiny loft and into something with a park view instead of the view of my fire escape and two different brick walls.

I tell her I'm in Northern California. I'm on vacation. She tells me she'll pick up the check for my red eye if I'll just promise to be sitting across from her desk in the morning to discuss details. The winter shows are just around the corner and they need me now. I realize that I'm hesitating. I say yes. She transfers me to her assistant. I give her my information, and she's going to book me a flight.

"Everything cool?" Shep nods toward my phone once I hang up. I'm still gripping it in my hand.

"Uh—yeah. Everything's fine."

"Good." He comes and sits on the coffee table opposite me. I peel off my coat. I didn't notice how much I was sweating until now. "Can we talk about what just happened back there?" He takes my chin in his hand and tilts my head up.

"What are you doing?"

"Looking at your pupils."

I shake free. My mind is racing, but I'm okay. "I'm fine," I tell him. I let out a deep breath and suck another back in. Again. "I'm sorry. I had another panic attack back there. I shouldn't have run off like that. I can't—I can't explain it. I just freaked out."

"I figured it was something like that. Listen we can spend the rest of the week in the house. I can call my bosses and tell them I need to forego a few days. I've sent them thousands of images."

"No—no. I don't want you to fuck up your project because of me. It's fine. I just—" I realize again what I'm saying. "I—Shep, I have to leave."

"I won't try and screw you outdoors again. I promise. And I'll take Titus out for quick walks and you can stay here. He'll be cranky about it, but it's only a few more days. He'll survive."

"No. Shep. It's not about that. I actually have to leave." I stand. "I, um, that was the editor-in-chief at Mode. She asked me to come work for her."

"Oh," he says. "That's good, right? My mom used to swaddle me in Mode." He lets out this laugh as he scrubs the back of his head. "My grandfather used to joke that she was always too Mode for these woods." I cringe at the way his face drops then, at the way he looks at me. "So you have to leave like right now?"

"She wants me to come in tomorrow. Her assistant is booking me a redeye out of Sacramento as we speak. I have to go," I say. A sort of clarity washes over me as the words come out of my mouth. It's not just clarity though. It's a sense of excitement. And there's hope for the first time in months. I want this job.

"Okay." Shep stands too. "Well I guess you should pack. It takes almost four hours to get to SMF and it's going to snow today. I'd take you, but you have the rental. Are you cool to drive?"

"Yes. I'm okay. I swear. Just a little jittery, but not like swerve off the road jittery."

"I meant with the snow."

"Oh, yeah. Fine." I wave him off. "I took driver's ed in the dead of winter. I'll be fine."

"Okay." Suddenly we both can't stand to look at each other.

"I should pack."

"Yeah."

He turns toward the kitchen and I head straight into the bedroom. My stuff is spilling out of my suitcase and I still have a ton of things cluttering up his bathroom sink. I start shoving things in side pockets. When I look up Shep is standing in the doorway of his bedroom with my toothbrush and my lotion in his hands. I stop and sit down on the bed.

"I'm sorry," I say.

"For what?" I don't miss how casual his voice suddenly is.

"For leaving like this. I fucking barge into your life. Twice! And now I'm like peace, bruh. It's been fun. After I have a complete meltdown on you in the middle of the woods. I'm such an asshole I actually want you to ask me stay." The last part comes out like straight vomit, but I can't take it back.

Shep doesn't seem to mind how crazy I clearly I am. How shitty. He sets my stuff down on the dresser and just leans back on the solid piece of wood. I watch the muscles in his forearms bulge as he folds them across his chest. He pins me with a cool stare.

"Why would I do that?"

"What?"

"I said, why would I do that? Why would I ask you to stay?" Shit. He's pissed.

"Sorry," I apologize again. "You're right. You wouldn't. Fuck, that was really shitty and selfish of me. You're right. Word vomit. I shouldn't have said that."

"And what if I did ask you to stay? It wouldn't make a lick of difference."

"Shep…"

"He's dead," he says.

"Who?"

"The bastard who tried to kill you. He's dead, Claudia. He's not lurking anywhere in these woods. He's dead. I killed him. And the man who hurt Miles is about to get the injection! They can't hurt you!" The words exploded out of him. I'm not sure he knows how loud he's shouting. I'm swallowing as if that will calm him down.

"I…I know that."

"No you don't. I didn't realize until just now, but I should have—the gun."

I groan and cover my face. I have completely fucked up this man's life. "Shep—"

"You know, there was a minute, like a split second where I felt really fucked up inside. I killed a man, but I had no choice. He gave me no choice. Right? I killed a guy. With that shotgun. For you. Because he was trying to hurt you. I didn't even know you, but he was trying to hurt you so I did what I had to do. And then you come back and I have this—this retroactive bloodlust. I'd do it again. I'd kill anyone who tried to hurt you. But you still don't feel safe with me."

"Jesus. Shep. That's not—none of this is on you. None of it. It's on those two pieces of shit and every once in a while I like to blame Miles for his horrible choice in vacation destinations, but none of this is your responsibility. God. You saved my life. You're off the hook!"

"I love you!"

My chest feels like it snaps so hard, my mouth clamps shut.

"I love you," he says again. "And that's not your fault, that is all me. But it's true and I am definitely on the hook."

And this is what I didn't want. Because I love him too, but I can't tell him that, because none of this is real. It's all temporary. I have to go back to my life and he has to go back to his. We can't pretend we didn't meet over my sliced scalp and the barrel of that blessed shotgun. We can't pretend that I didn't just sprint like a mad woman through the woods to get away from the ghost of my almost killer and maybe even Shep himself, not fifteen minutes before. I'm too fucked up for him. Too messy.

He deserves better. Someone who can give him everything, a fresh start. Trauma free. I love him, but that will never be me.

"Don't forget your charger. It's still in the wall right there."

I glance at the outlet on my side of the bed, then back at him. He's walking out the door. "Shep."

"Yeah?"

There's nothing I can say. Nothing I can do to fix this. I need to leave this man alone so he can finally get on with his life without me twisting and fucking everything up.

He nods, like he knows. I'm not woman enough for him. I'm too chickenshit to be what he needs. "Don't worry about it," he says. "I know you're a pro behind the wheel, but driving down is still tricky even in good weather. Let me know when you're ready to go. You can follow me back down." He doesn't wait for me to respond. He just walks out of the bedroom. A few seconds later I hear the front door slam.

CHAPTER SEVENTEEN

SHEP

I don't punch any trees, but I do all the pacing I can and by the time Claudia comes out on the porch and lets me know she's ready to go, my blood pressure is somewhat back to normal. It's a dick move, but I don't say goodbye the way I should. I don't kiss her. I don't hug her. I don't push her hair off her face one more time and touch the end of that scar on her forehead. I don't wrap her in my arms and tell her what I really think of her or how the real her makes me feel, not just the version of her that's been living in my head for the last six months.

I don't tell her we're cool or that I understand. I don't say that it is a big deal that she's splitting early. She would have been leaving in a few days anyway, but we're not cool and I'll never understand what the fuck just happened between us and why I think she owes me anything. It's better if I keep my fucking mouth shut and let her be on her way. I don't tell her that she should have just left me the fuck alone.

I just climb behind the wheel of my truck and wait for her to get into her rental. It hasn't started snowing yet, but I still go slow as we drive down to the bottom of the mountain and then pull over to the side of the road and wave her on. She pulls up beside me and stops. I see her roll down her window. I roll down mine, but I have nothing to say to her.

"I'll call you before I take off," she says.

I want to tell her she doesn't need to. She doesn't need to check in with me. I'm not her next of kin or her emergency contact. Where she goes from here is none of my business. She has friends who she can check in with. She should call them. But I don't tell her that. I say okay and tell her to drive safe. She's smart and doesn't draw this shit out a moment longer. She drives away. It starts snowing on my way back up the mountain.

Claudia knows better than to call me before her flight takes off. Maybe she doesn't want to hear my voice. I don't want to hear hers. I don't want to hear anything she has to say. She sends me a text instead.

Taking off in five.
Thank you for letting me stay.

I text her back right away. We're not leaving room for second guessing.

Safe travels.

I don't hear from her again.

I drink for almost three days. It doesn't snow much and what does fall melts when the temperature suddenly rises and the snow turns to rain. I don't drive anywhere and I know where to avoid ravines and steep falls when I take Titus stumbling through the woods. I come to a few conclusions, mostly that I don't know what the fuck I was thinking. My dick isn't a magic wand. I wasn't going to save her. I wasn't going to heal her with my kisses or however much I decided to jizz all over her back. And I sure as fuck wasn't going to fix myself.

Friday morning, I'm out of whisky. After I finish my morning expedition, send off my images, and sit through two conference calls that could have been emails, I feel like I should go down to pick up more alcohol. Spending the weekend in a nearly blacked out state is the best plan I can come up with. I send off some assets for review and try to clear my head long enough to find my jacket. I'm looking for my keys when my cellphone rings. It's May-Bell.

"Saint?" she says bashfully and I know she feels bad. She hasn't called me that in years. She's testing the waters to see if I'll hang up on her.

"Hey, May," I reply.

"Neither of us are much for hem and haw, so I'll just get right to the point. Jad and I are really sorry about what happened the other night. I know Claudia is heading out soon, but we were hoping you two would stop by for lunch before she has to go. We want to apologize to her and you. Properly."

"She already left," I say.

"Oh. We just missed her?"

"No. She left on Tuesday."

"Oh! Thought she was staying 'til the weekend. Why did she leave early? It wasn't because of us, was it?"

"No, May. She had to get back for a job interview."

"Oh. Well good. She said she was looking."

"Mhmm," I say. There's dead air on May-Bell's end for a few seconds.

"Is she coming back?" she asks.

"No." Sure, anything is possible, but we both know how this is really going to play out.

"I'm sorry, darling. I know you two went through a lot together. And I know you must care about her a lot to invite her into your life like that."

"Yeah." There's another silence and then I hear Jad mumbling something in the background.

"Well Jad's gonna come by anyway and bring you your chainsaw and I'll send him over with something for you to eat."

"Okay." I take that as a sign that maybe I don't need to go into town for more liquor. "I'll be here."

"Okay." I hang up with May-Bell and give up looking for my keys. I snap for Titus to come and watch him from the porch while he sniffs around the yard until Jad pulls up.

"How long you been sitting there?" he asks.

"Since I hung up with May."

"You waiting for me?"

"Yep."

"Am I banned from your house now?"

"No, just giving T some exercise."

"Ah. Should have brought Fox by. Next time." He comes over to the steps and I hear at least three of his joints crack as he groans and sits down beside me. He's quiet for a while. I think he's going to launch into some speech about the weather or act like everything's cool and ask if I want to go fishing, but he doesn't.

"Man to man, I was out of line, Shep. And I'm sorry for that."

I nod and watch Titus try to pick up a clump of dirt with his paw. "I appreciate that, Jad."

"I was worried about you and I got a little ahead of myself. Can't promise it won't happen again 'cause it's a little hard to unlearn pigheadedness at my age, but I am sorry."

I chuckle a bit and shake my head. "I appreciate the honesty too."

"I don't care much for Sarah still. If that wasn't obvious."

"It wasn't actually."

"What?" He looks over at me as I shrug.

"I'm pretty sure, or at least I *was*, that everyone blamed me for not making it work with Sarah."

"In a place like this it might feel like you belong with the girl next door, but that ain't always the case."

"True." I let Titus walk a few feet too far into the woods before I whistle for him. He comes trotting back to the porch. He knows he's been caught. I scratch his head then Jad gets a turn and Titus tries to lick his palm.

"I know, I'm not your dad and I'm not Egil, but May-Bell and I love you just like you're our boy. When you showed up May and I decided to give all the love we had that we weren't spreading around to you. You ever wonder why we ain't got no kids of our own?"

"You're too cantankerous to conceive?"

"Close. I can't. It's me. Plumbing don't work. Never did, but May didn't leave me. And back long before it was hip to tell people you just didn't want to have kids, May told people it was her. She did that for me. She didn't have to, but she knew how awful I felt that I couldn't give her youngins so she tried to save my pride. I didn't let her keep that up for more than five minutes, but that was when I knew her and I were a team. We loved each other that much. And we keep trying to protect each other."

I look over at him when the emotion starts choking up his voice. "You deserve that, Shepard. You hear me? You deserve whoever is gonna look out for you the way you look out for them. Not someone who's going to turn on you when you don't see eye to eye. You deserve someone who's gonna stick around for you." He lets out a harsh breath, then swallows the lump in his throat. He's close to crying. So am I, but we both manage to keep it in.

"So what do you think I should do?" I ask. "You think I should sell this place and leave?"

"Not if you don't want to. Get on the internet. That's what it's for, right? Make you a dating profile. Maybe there's some nice conservationist in Montana who's looking to move further west. Find someone who works for you. Stop trying to make these girls fit your life up here. It's not gonna work."

"You're right." I know he is.

"I'm sorry things didn't work out with Claudia though. She did seem like a very nice girl. Very pretty too."

"I won't tell May-Bell you said."

"Oh, she agrees. That was the first thing *she* said about her."

"I see."

"We square, you and I?" He holds out his hand.

"Yeah. We're good." I shake it.

"Good. Come on by for dinner tonight. I know you Olsen men are keen on your lonely commiserating, but you smell like a distillery and I think you could go for some good food."

"Okay."

"Now come on." He slaps me on my knee and nods toward the bed of his truck.

"Come get your chainsaw."

CHAPTER EIGHTEEN

CLAUDIA

45 Days Later

I need to stop looking at my phone while I'm walking. I've walked into three people already today, two of them between the train and my building. And maybe if I were paying a little bit more attention I would see Liz standing at my door when I come out of the elevator. I would have enough time to make a break for the stairs.

She coughs to catch my attention and when I look up I'm only two feet away from her. She's standing there holding a bottle of rosé and the look on her face tells me she will chase me down and tackle me if I try to escape. I haven't seen her or any of my friends since I got back.

"Heeey," I say as I slow to a complete stop.

She shakes her head with that are you fucking kidding me look. "Where do I start, Claudia?"

"Uh—"

"You never take my calls. You've barely responded to any of my or Brook or the girls' texts? You blew Rayna off on her birthday and you look like complete shit."

"This is Gucci, thank you very much."

"Well it looks like you and Gucci haven't eaten real food in two weeks."

"Would you like to come inside?" I ask. She's nowhere near done cussing me out, but we don't need to do this in my hallway.

"How sweet of you! Of course I would." I roll my eyes and nudge by her so I can unlock the door. I head straight inside. I set my things down and go right for the drawer where I keep the corkscrew. I turn around and hand it to her before I pull off my jacket. She sets it and the rosé down, takes off her own coat. I grab some wine glasses and walk over to the couch. She's right behind me.

"You'd think we were friends," she says under her breath.

"I've been busy."

"Claudia."

"What?!"

"Do. Not," she says in her best mom tone. "I'm not the one. Okay, bitch? I want to know exactly what happened out there with the mountain man and I want to know exactly what you've been doing since you got back. I know Mode is the real deal, but I refuse to believe you don't have time to see me, like ever."

"Liz."

She doesn't budge. She just crosses her arms and glares right back at me. "Try again."

"Fine." I throw up my hands. "Where do you want me to start? With the fact that I'm pretty sure I had a psychotic break and decided not to seek help for it or with the fact that Shep is the most amazing man I have ever met in my entire life and he professed his love to me before I threw up the two fingers and left him hanging so I could rush back here to meet Vivianne. And I don't know, how about I sprinkle in a little of how I feel like I don't think I know how to process basic human emotions anymore."

Her mouth drops open. "Oh babe."

"Or maybe we can talk about how I lost my shit up there like a minimum of five times and he handled it perfectly. And I'm not talking like a perfect medical professional. I'm talking marriage material, this is how you want a man to hold you for the rest of your life type shit. Like you know he can handle anything you throw at him, calm and cool."

"Babe."

"Work is kicking my ass. Kleinman's was a walk in the park compared to Mode. Vivianne is a genius and she is demanding as fuck, but you're right. I'm not working all the time. I just feel like I can't slow down."

"Why not?"

"Cause I'll want to call him, I'll want to *see* him. Cause I'll lose my shit again. Cause I'll have to face the fact that I'm still in fucking agony over Miles and I somehow managed to just pile on when it comes to Shep. I should have never gone out there. I feel like if I can't see him I might as well avoid everyone and everything else."

"Damn," Liz says as she lets out a big breath. She opens the rosé and pours us both a healthy glass. We both take large sips. It warms my chest and I feel my body start to really heat for the first time in weeks. I hate it. "How do you feel about him? Really."

"I don't know. I feel crazy. That's how I feel."

"Why? Why do you feel crazy?"

"Because I love him," I say honestly and the fat tears come. "I really wasn't trying to ignore you and the girls. I just, anything but work feels like too much right now."

More tears. Silent, but still streaming down my face. Liz grabs the box of tissues off my coffee table. I grab a few from the box but I don't bother to wipe my face. "I quit Kleinman's because I felt like I could never come to work again without people whispering about me. Do you know how weird it feels to know that people are constantly telling every new person who gets hired that you were almost murdered?

"Like everyone was so nice and sympathetic, but no one could treat me like myself. I felt like a movie of the week. I was so *angry*. I loved working there and no one would just let me go back to work. I just wanted to feel like myself again. I just wanted to be myself and no one there would let me."

"And Shep made you feel like yourself again?"

"He made me feel like I am different now and that's... expected."

Liz reaches over and squeezes my hand. "Babe, it is. I wasn't the same after I lost my parents. I'll never be that girl again. Same with Brook. Some things about her are the same, but she was very different from the person you know now. Loss like that does change you. You know that."

"Yeah. He's a part of the orphan club too. And he said some things about having to shoot that guy to protect me. I think it really fucked him up."

"See!"

I laugh and wipe my face. "There was the sex too."

"Oh thank god. I was worried for a second. Three thousand miles is way too far to travel for no sex. Tell me literally everything." I do. Or at least I give her the general overview and some of the dirtier details. I see nearly every emotion pass over her face by the time I get to the bondage and the flogging. And then I tell her about Sarah.

"I think he found something in me he couldn't find in her and then I just left him. It sucks. He's amazing and he's just up there all alone. With his dog. And he is married to that mountain. I don't think I could ask him to come here to visit. He thrives off fresh mountain air. The smell of the subway alone would kill him."

She sighs. "That is tough, but you're... you're not responsible for him in that way," she says with a little grimace.

"I know. I know you're right. But—"

"But you really have feelings for this guy?"

"I think I do and they are so fucking complicated. Did I Florence Nightingale a dude because he saved me or do I really love *him*?" I grab my phone and pull up the pictures that I've been purposefully avoiding for weeks. I hand Liz my phone. She gasps and then makes an awwwing noise.

"Laudi, you two look so cute."

I groan and sit back against the corner of my couch. "There's more." I take my phone back and pull up the emails Shep sent me. I show her all the pictures he took of just me. I watch Liz as her eyes grow wide.

"He took these?"

"Yeah."

"Oh. Girl."

"I know."

"First of all he's a really good photographer and second—"

"I *know*. You don't have to say it."

"I mean... he like, loves you. Like looooves you."

"It's that obvious, isn't it? And he doesn't even photograph people usually. Just nature. I spent the entire flight back looking at these, crying. I was so lucky no one was sitting next to me."

"Have you heard from him?"

"He emailed me these, but that's it. It was a blank email with just the pictures." I pull up the photo he took of me and Titus that morning in the clearing.

"Oh yeah. He's turning into Hemingway up there over these pics."

I laugh, but more tears leak out of the corners of my eyes. I wipe my face this time. "I don't know what to do."

"Here's the advice I'm going to give you. First of all, don't ever avoid me again. Vivianne loves me. I will show up at your job. I'll bring Brook. You don't want that."

"God. No I don't."

"No you don't. Second of all. I think you need to talk to someone. Find a new therapist. I agree, whatsherface sucked and you weren't clicking with her anyway. Find someone you want to talk to and take care of yourself."

"And thirdly?"

She holds up her hands. "Oh no thirdly. I can't help you there."

"Gee. Thanks."

"You think I'm going to tell you to run after him? Nah. We're not that drunk yet."

I laugh and reach for my wine.

"I'm too selfish to tell you to move to bumfuck Northern California and I would never tell you to leave Mode for a dude. Never. That's crazy, but I think you are feeling a lot and I think you are hurting. Maybe if you talk to someone you can sort out what's really going on and you can see if you really do love him, all this other shit aside."

I let out a deep breath as more tears roll down my cheeks. She's right.

"In the meantime, I'm gonna order us some pizza and you're going to eat. I know you probably had a carrot and some champagne today and I know there's an image at Mode, but we are both thick women and we are beautiful that way."

"Amen," I say. "Extra pepperoni, please."

"Coming right up."

SHEP

The morning of the third Saturday in December, I get a phone call. It's Connie calling me from the diner.

"Morning, Shep. I'm glad I caught you," she says.

"Everything okay?" I ask her.

"Yeah, honey. Everything's fine. Listen, I was going to try to come up with something clever or cute to get you down here, but I'm not sure that's a good idea. Claudia's here. She said she was going to drive right up to your place, but she doesn't know how to get up there. And she said she would have called you herself, but you two aren't exactly speaking so she didn't know if you would answer the phone. She also said she knows about the mess with Sarah and asked me to keep that last part to myself, which I will."

"I—okay."

"You want to come on down or I can have Jerry guide her up to your place." She pauses. "Or I can ask her to leave. It's your call, sweetheart."

My brain flatlines for a second. I have no fucking clue what to say, but then I remember I still have Connie waiting for a response. "I'll, uh. I'll be down in a bit. Thanks, Connie."

"No problem. We'll see you soon."

I try not to spend the entire drive down attempting to figure out what the hell she could possibly be doing here. I tell myself whatever she wants, handle it down there. Don't let her back up to my place. I can't do this shit with her. Hear her out, whatever she needs to say. And then it occurs to me. She's pregnant. I almost drive off the road when I realize I've pushed the gas to the floor. I get to Connie's in record time and almost sideswipe Rich's car when I pull into the lot. I take the stairs five at once and almost rip the door off the hinges. The bell rings loud as hell as it smacks against the frame. I scare the shit out of Connie.

"Hey. Sorry. She still here?"

"Yeah." Connie points to the back. I whip around and there is Claudia standing next to my favorite booth. She looks the same, but totally different. She's wearing this thick fancy beige trench coat that's made out of some warm looking material and a full face of makeup. She's wearing fuck me black boots with heels that make her a half foot taller, but to hell with all of that. I look right at her stomach and I take the entire length of the diner in three steps.

"Are you pregnant?"

Her head jerks back and she frowns. "No. Why?"

"Oh." I exhale. "Okay."

"Did you *think* you got me pregnant?"

"No, but it was the only reason I could think for you to come back."

"Ah, oh. Yeah I guess that makes sense. Would you like to sit down?"

"Yeah, sure." Sitting is a good idea. I'm about to pass out. We both sit in the booth. I pull off my skull cap and take a sip from one of the waters sitting in the middle of the table.

"You okay?" she asks me.

"No. Not really. What's up?"

"Right. It's nice to see you, but from the look on your face I'm not sure you feel the same way. I'll spare you any more suspense."

"Please. What are you doing here?"

"I love you and I'm hoping you still love me too."

I think my eye twitches, but I'm not sure. I've spent the last two months trying to work this woman out of my system. Two months trying to meet people. Trying to date. Even doing weird things like bar hopping in San Francisco. Unless she wants to marry me right now, I don't have time to hop back on this carousel of *I'm not quite sure* with her. She's staring at me. She wants an answer. I don't have one.

"Why?" I say.

"Why do I hope you still love me? From time to time, it can be...beneficial for both parties when feelings are reciprocated?" she says like I'm the one who's lost my mind. "Would this conversation work better if I popped out a tit or two?" She reaches for the belt on her jacket.

"No, please. Keep the tits in. I just want to know what you want. What changed?"

"I want you."

"But?"

"There is no but. I want to be with you."

"Here? Because this is where I live. This is my home and I'm not sure this is the best place for you."

"And two months ago I would have agreed with you, but that was before my friend cornered me and made me go back to seeing a therapist."

"And they told you to move out here with me?"

"God, you are still cranky as fuck. No. She told me that I have to actually process things. And she told me that I have to accept trauma and loss and learn that I can still thrive despite them." She wiggles in her seat and starts undoing her jacket anyway, but she keeps her sweater in place.

"Here's the thing. There's Before Claudia and there's After Claudia and I'll be After Claudia for the rest of my life. And After Claudia loves you. After Claudia loves being around you. After Claudia loves pushing your buttons. After Claudia has no idea how to go the rest of her life without being with you."

"What about your job? There's nothing in fashion up here. You've been to the boot store."

"Oh I'm keeping the job. I may have lied to my boss a little bit."

"Oh?" I don't like the sound of that.

"I told them we were getting married, but you have to stay here because you work for the forest service, which you technically do. I figure you are actually pretty accustomed to your alone time. Having any other person around twenty-four seven, even if that person is as beautiful and lovable as me would drive you crazy.

"I can telecommute from here a couple weeks out of the month and head back to the offices in New York the rest of the month. My whole job with Kleinman's was travel. I'm used to it. I've been to Paris twice since the last time I saw you. Also my therapist does Facetime sessions so when I'm here I can still keep up with our appointments," she says matter of factly like I should be impressed with this plan, which I am, but I'm still pretty fucking pissed off.

"Uh huh and what if I told you I was over you and your wishy-washy bullshit and there's no way I want to get together with you, let alone move you into my house two weeks out of the month."

"I'd sick Jad and May-Bell on you. Tell them you wasted a perfectly good proposal from a smart, beautiful, gracious woman who wants to put up with your stubborn, cranky shit voluntarily."

"They know you're here?"

"May-Bell was here when I pulled up."

"Great. So that's that?" I say. "We're getting married. End of story?"

"We don't have to get married right away, but I know what I want and I think it's stupid to pretend there's something better for me waiting back in the city."

"Mhmm." I roll my tongue around in my mouth and try not to bite a chunk out of the inside of my lip. She has a shitload of nerve. "You and this therapist really worked everything out. That's good. That's good."

"Okay." She puts her palms on the table. I glance down at the manicured nails that look like they cost a few thousand dollars before I look back up at her face. "I can see that I have fucked up the presentation a little bit and now you're angry. I get it. That was not entirely smooth or appealing. I'm being a little pushy, but I'm going to try and not make this worse. I am going to sit here and if you want me to get out of your life I think… you should be the one to leave this time.

"I'm not gonna tell you I regret coming here, because I don't. I don't think I made a mistake trying to see you. I do love you. I love you so much, Shep. I don't want you to tell me to go. I'm not even suggesting you do that. So I'm just going to sit here and maybe we can have breakfast together and talk about a future together. Like how I am definitely not pregnant. I don't think I'm ready for kids at all right now, but I think you'd make an awesome stay-at-home dad in five to six years if that's something that's crossed your mind. We can also talk about how we should both learn to whittle and how outdoor sex is still out of the question, but I would love to learn how to shoot. Or you can leave and I'll never bother you again."

I consider her for a moment. I look at those deep hazel eyes and that golden brown skin and whatever the fuck is on her mouth that makes me just want to shove my cock in it so she'll stop talking. I stand and head for the door. I feel everyone's eyes on me and I avoid Connie's gaze as she tracks my every move. I grab the handle, then turn back toward the booth. I see her head drop forward before I call out.

"Hey!"

She whips her head around, and her suddenly red rimmed eyes focus on me.

"You coming?" She stares at me a beat longer as I nod toward the parking lot. "I have plenty of bacon and carbs up at my place. No offense, Con. You know I think your food is amazing."

Connie laughs. "I do, honey."

I hold out my hand and it seems like forever before Claudia makes it back to me and laces her fingers with mine. I let her lead the way down the stairs and then I pull her into my arms and kiss the top of her head. She smells amazing.

"You really think I'm going to wait another two some-odd hours before I fuck my future wife again."

"Shep."

"It was the stay-at-home dad thing that really sold it," I say.

I feel her whole body shake as she laughs. "Should have led with that." She tilts her head up and rests her chin against my chest. I wipe her tears away with my thumbs and kiss that scar on her forehead. I'm never letting her go.

THE END

Keep an eye out for more give and take in...

SANCTUARY

Beards & Bondage 2
Coming Summer 2017

ACKNOWLEDGEMENTS

A whole village helped me finish this book, a whole dang village. Thank you to my parents, and my brother and sister for their continued to support. The ladies at The Ripped Bodice for the free wifi and the bomb diggity, fem positive lady space to write my words. Sarah, the best deadline partner on Earth. Alisha, Alyssa, Bree (and Donna by proxy), Courtney, Janet, Jenn, Bea and Carrie for the unwavering encouragement. A special thanks to Leah for helping me name almost every character in this book. All the love and kisses to my editor, Tara and my cover artist, TL. A huge thank you to my readers who keep coming back for more and bringing your friends and family members to my books. You guys rock.

And thank you to the government employees at the Forest Service, the National Park Service and many others who continue to run renegade social media accounts in the name of truth, science, nature, and common sense. The science help feeds the art and we appreciate you.

ABOUT THE AUTHOR

Rebekah was raised in Southern New Hampshire and now lives in Southern California where she finally found her love for writing romance.

Her interests include Wonder Woman collectibles, cookies, James Taylor, whatever Nicki Minaj is doing at any given moment, quality hip-hop, football, American muscle cars, large breed dogs, and the ocean. When she's not working, writing, reading, or sleeping, she is watching HGTV and cartoons, or taking dance classes. If given the chance, she will cheat at UNO.

Come on by and get to know Rebekah on her twitter at @rdotspoon. You also can find more stories by Rebekah at rebekahweatherspoon.com

Made in the USA
Monee, IL
13 August 2021